NEURODANCER

A <u>LIQUID COOL</u> CYBERPUNK DETECTIVE NOVEL

Book Three

AUSTIN DRAGON

Published by Well-Tailored Books, California

NeuroDancer
(Liquid Cool, Book 3)

978-1-946590-56-5 (paperback)
978-1-946590-50-3 (ebook)

http://www.austindragon.com

Book cover design by Whendell Souza

Printed in the United States of America

CONTENTS

PART ONE | The Dame 7

Chapter 1 | Client Zero 2

Chapter 2 | The Traffic Cop 4

Chapter 3 | The Good Kosher Man 8

Chapter 4 | The Attorney 13

Chapter 5 | Pops 17

Chapter 6 | Dog Man 19

Chapter 7 | Flash 21

Chapter 8 | Punch Judy 23

PART TWO | The Movie-Town Metropolis Case 25

Chapter 9 | China Doll 26

Chapter 10 The Man From the Studio 29

Chapter 11 | The Movie Mogul 32

Chapter 12 | Beat Box 37

Chapter 13 | Mr. Meta 43

Chapter 14 | Mr. Caret 44

Chapter 15 | NeuroDancer 48

Chapter 16 | Rogue One 50

PART THREE | The Man of the Galaxy Case 52

Chapter 17 | Officers Bus and Boot 53

Chapter 18 | Logo 56

Chapter 19 | The Politician 59

Chapter 20 | The House of Jed 62

Chapter 21 | NeuroDancer 66

Chapter 22 | Rogue Two 68

PART FOUR | The Five Rings of Babel Case................................70

Chapter 23 | China Doll...71

Chapter 24 | Caret Senior..73

Chapter 25 | Caret...76

Chapter 26 | Logo...79

Chapter 27 | The Men From OC..82

Chapter 28 | Punch Judy...86

Chapter 29 | Beta Max...88

Chapter 30 | Bite-Size..92

Chapter 31 | Beta Max...96

PART FIVE | The Gangsters of SAG..97

Chapter 32 | Union Hovertruckers 98

Chapter 33 | Tuck Rogers and Perfect Tony 102

Chapter 34 | The Politician... 107

Chapter 35 | China Doll.. 110

Chapter 36 | Master Jed... 113

Chapter 37 | Caret... 116

Chapter 38 | Logo.. 119

Chapter 39 | Rogue Three.. 122

Chapter 40 | Punch Judy.. 125

Chapter 41 | Tuck Rogers and Perfect Tony 127

Chapter 42 | SAG... 132

Chapter 43 | Bite-Size... 139

Chapter 44 | The Oldest Man on Earth 142

Chapter 45 | Chief Hub 147

Chapter 46 | Caret... 149

Chapter 47 | Madness... 150

PART SIX | Prime Numbers.. 154

Chapter 48 | China Doll: The Chronicle of the Wife 155

Chapter 49 | The Peanut Gallery 160

Chapter 50 | Wilford Jr. 165

Chapter 51 | The Chronicle of Jed 170

Chapter 52 | Jed 176

Chapter 53 | The Mayor 180

Chapter 54 | The Visitor 187

Chapter 55 | Mrs. Meta 193

Chapter 56 | All the Kings Men 199

Chapter 57 | The Election Lady 206

PART SEVEN | Virtual Games 211

Chapter 58 | NeuroDancer 212

Chapter 59 | Tag 219

Chapter 60 | Beta Max 223

Chapter 61 | Mr. Incom 236

Chapter 62 | Cyberpunks 238

PART EIGHT | Smoking Rooms, Booze Bottles, and Laser Guns 241

Chapter 63 | Caret 242

Chapter 64 | Logo 248

Chapter 65 | Beta Max 253

Chapter 66 | The Knight, the Captain and the President 257

Chapter 67 | Cruz, the Interrogator 263

PART NINE | A Dame to Die For 265

Chapter 68 | I, Executioner... 266

Chapter 69 | The NeuroDancer.. 268

<u>Introduction</u>

To be a freelance private detective in the supercity of Metropolis. Not owned by any uber-government agency, megacorporation, or shadowy criminal cartel. That was the status I enjoyed, after more than a few deadly dangerous cases in the relatively short tenure of my Liquid Cool Detective Agency.

But I didn't want to be known for my gunplay or getting shot—the latter a skill I seemed to excel at. I wanted to be known for *not* using my gun—brain work. Feline cases were what I called them; I had had plenty of canine cases with everybody trying to kill me, bullets and lasers flying. I wanted to be the suave, sophisticated operator to go after the butt-in-chair, Japanese-whiskey-in-hand, brainiac criminals. Anyone could go after the crazy maniacs. I wanted to do battle against a higher class of criminals. Why should the big corporate detective firms corner that market? I wanted to show off my intellectual skills and prove this private street detective wasn't the stereotypical doofus.

My last case of the Blade Gunner had given me such a strong desire to avoid any outrageous violence and frenzy for a while. Unfortunately, in Metropolis, there would be no such luck for me, as the case of the *NeuroDancer* would prove.

I was a permanent cosmic magnet for violence. The violence didn't have to be overt. Subtle violence—quiet, plotting criminals—could kill you as effectively as killer terminator robots and supercyborgs. I was accustomed to the hulking, scary-looking, skin-crawl-inducing criminals. But I had learned the hard way that they could wear silky nylons and neon lipstick, too.

Which is crazier, indeed: the criminal—or the client?

PART ONE

The Dame

CHAPTER 1

Client Zero

The only sound was that of the rain hitting the window behind me. As I sat behind my desk, I knew I was in trouble from the moment she walked into my office. The high-fashion, two-piece black slicker outfit she wore was tight enough to be a second skin, and wrapped around her eyes was a clear red visor. Those piercing eyes locked on me and never let go.

The Dame sat in the chair directly facing me and crossed her legs.

"Mr. Cruz, I'd like to hire you," she said in her sensual voice.

"Miss, I gotta ask. Is it dangerous?"

"Dangerous, Mr. Cruz?"

"Yeah. What do you want to hire me to do? Does it involve...gangsters? Cyborgs? Killer robots? I don't do dangerous. Dangerous means I get shot. I don't like to get shot."

"Oh, no, Mr. Cruz. I'm just an innocent damsel in distress, who needs a little help from the local private detective."

I said to myself, *Yeah, sure*. I knew I wasn't gonna touch this case with a 10-foot pole. It had danger written all over it, back and front.

"Miss, I'm sorry, but I actually won't be able to take your case. I—"

"Oh, I forgot one thing, Mr. Cruz," the NeuroDancer added.

"What's that?" I asked.

The only thing my eyes focused on was the slim briefcase she opened and laid on top of my desk. It was filled with stacks of beautiful currency.

"When do you want me to start?" I asked.

CHAPTER 2

The Traffic Cop

My name is Cruz. I was born, raised, have lived, and expect to expire in the supercity of Metropolis. Fifty million people, 200-story megaskyscrapers, hovercars everywhere, and a rain that almost never stopped. This was my life as a private detective at Liquid Cool—solving crimes and dealing with low-life criminals in a high-tech world.

Today, however, was "get the errands done before wedding weekend" day. I did something I'd almost never done before—overslept. A late start meant I'd be doing errands until late in the night.

Another thing happened that had almost never happened before—I was pulled over by a traffic cop. I glanced at the display of my Ford Pony. Yeah, I was speeding, but no faster than anyone else, even though with my hovervehicle, I could more than drive faster than anyone else.

I drove a red, classic Ford Pony—high-performance, supercharged, advanced nitro-acceleration hydrogen engine. I had built it from a junkyard shell over 15 years ago, part by part, as a kid. It made the mouths of the genuine hovercar enthusiasts and collectors hang open and had been featured—without my permission—in so many hovercar magazines that I had lost count. But I was no speedster.

Being pulled over for a traffic stop was no simple thing. Sky traffic never stopped in any city, but Metropolis was not any city—it was the largest supercity on Earth. It was not fair to say the rain never stopped, because sometimes it did, but sky traffic never stopped. It had to flow, because even the slowest hoverjalopy was still a flying craft that, though it had vertical lift and hovering capability, was meant to fly forward. If you were pulled over, you had to pull out of the sky lane and descend to a temporary holding pad—usually on top of a nearby monolith building.

The traffic hovercruiser still had its lights flashing when we both touched down on the pad. Metro Police had long ago separated general beat cop patrol from traffic patrol. With our supercity's population, it probably wouldn't have been wise to expect the meter maid to also shoot it out with bank robbers, or expect heavy policetroopers to chase someone down for a busted taillight. Beat cops did their work. Traffic cops did theirs.

The cop—I didn't consider traffic to be real police—exited his cruiser and slowly walked to me with his chest light on. My driver's side window was already down, with my left hand holding out my ID, my right hand on the steering wheel. I knew the drill. A hovertarp floated above us to keep most of the rain off us.

He peeked in and took my ID from my hand.

"Do you know why I stopped you, sir?"

"I was speeding, officer," I answered.

"Why might you be doing that?"

"Well, officer, I was in a hurry to get about my errands of the day and didn't watch my speed."

"Is all the information on your ID current?"

"Yes, officer."

He took my ID and started back to his cruiser.

I had never understood people who were rude or crazy when stopped by police. If they had been a police intern like I'd been in high school, they would know every police officer, street or traffic, wanted you to give them any excuse *not* to have to write you a ticket. Tickets meant the headache of more paperwork. Arrest, yes. Tickets, no. Smile, say "sir" or "ma'am," and most would let you go.

My focus was on my side-view mirror, because the traffic cop had stopped on his way to his cruiser and was walking back to my open window.

"You're Cruz, the detective?"

He was no longer standing to the side but right at the open driver's side window.

"That's me."

"Wilford Jr.'s friend?"

"Yes, the sergeant is a buddy."

"Why didn't you say so?" He handed me back my ID.

I smiled. I was home free, or so I thought. The traffic cop leaned down, looking in my back seat.

"Mr. Cruz, what's that?" He pointed with his leather-gloved hand.

I closed my eyes, because I realized what he had noticed.

"It's not what you think, Officer."

"Mr. Cruz, I want to be your friend, since you're a friend to cops and do the right thing, but I see a big ol' fat box of illegal wet wipes on the backseat of your vehicle. Do you have the proper permit for them?"

I sighed. If I had only put them in the trunk, which the street vendor had told me to do, I wouldn't be in this situation.

"Officer, you caught me. It's actually for my building. You might have heard about that 'incident' at the Concrete Mama in Rabbit City, the 'incident' that no one is supposed to know about. We got all those C-4 explosives out of there, but we have a lot of damage to clean up. We need the wet wipes."

"Mr. Cruz, I'm going to ignore what you said, because I must have mistakenly heard you say the residents of your residential tower are illegally hoarding wet wipes without a permit. Mr. Cruz, do you know why you need a permit for wet wipes?"

"Because they can destroy the Metro sewer system."

"Mr. Cruz, not all laws are good, but every once in a while, a few slip through that make more than damn sense. Everyone wants to use those convenient wet wipes, but somehow, they manage to get into the sewer rather than the trash chute. All those wet wipes fuse together and form a substance more solid than steel, rock, titanium, platinum, and Kryptonite put together. That pressure gets blocked, then before you know it, a pipe explodes and kills some poor family or takes out their entire apartment."

"Could I get a warning, officer?"

"Mr. Cruz, I can only let a citizen slide on one crime per stop. Let me walk back to my cruiser and write you your ticket for the illegal wet wipes. I don't do warnings. If I do it, I do it for real. Writing a ticket, or shooting a perp, I do it for real."

Yep, that's how all Metro police were, even the traffic cops.

CHAPTER 3

The Good Kosher Man

I could no longer say I had never gotten a ticket in my life. I hated that! I was not going to let it go. I'd pay the ticket, go to court, do community service, whatever I needed to do, but I was going to have the ticket expunged from my record. My secretary was the felon. I was going to remain the squeaky-clean one, even though I had shot plenty of bad guys—only because they had shot at me, or were going to—except for one of them, who was unarmed, but he was the one who had put all those C-4 explosives in my residential tower to blow us all up.

Imagine if I ever had my record run again. Illegal possession and transportation of wet wipes. That was like back when I was an intern, and in class, the officers were recalling the weirdest arrests they'd ever made. One was when two traffic cops arrested a male and female suspect going at it in the backseat of their hovercar—but there was only one person. The class erupted in laughter, and when another intern said aloud, "I don't understand," you had a class on the floor holding their stomachs, because they were laughing so hard.

That's how it was going to be for me if I didn't get that ticket off my record. I was known in Metropolis. If I were just some Average Joe, then I would have forgotten it, and let it stand—but how was it going to look that the famous private street detective was some kind of wet wipe bootlegger? Police would just laugh. I couldn't let my reputation be tarnished like that.

Good Kosher didn't do pick-up service. There was no "call in your order and have it waiting for you by the parking lot elevators." Most markets had a premier service, but not the owner, Mr. Watts. He'd say, "I have to grow your food, maintain it, pick it, clean it, package it, and deliver it to you, too? If you're too lazy to come into my store to get your own food, then stay at home and starve."

Only Good Kosher could get away with that philosophy—but when you're in high demand, with highly desired goods and services, you write the rules. I loved that it was a long-established generational business, that didn't change their way of doing business despite market pressures, and so did all their regular customers like me.

My task was simple: load up on everything Dot and I might need for after the wedding. Honeymoon food service in the bungalow for one night, maybe a day, was one thing, but since we'd be there a week, we still had to live. We were going to be in Bliss Resort, and prices in that part of Metropolis were beyond crazy. I was a famous detective, but I wasn't rich. Even if I were rich, I wouldn't pay what they wanted. Splurge for one night, maybe a day, only. Beyond that, the place had a full refrigerator and freezer, and they were going to get thoroughly used.

Besides food, I had to come to grips with the fact that I was going to be staying in a foreign place, not the Concrete Mama, or my parents'. First, I had my germophobia, which had to be managed. Second, I vividly remembered hotel suite crime scenes, where the CSI kid waves an ultraviolet light wand in a darkened room and you see all the glowing body fluids everywhere—even after the room had supposedly been thoroughly scrubbed clean, daily. Nasty!

I was going to stock up on all the commercial-strength cleaning supplies, and even if I had to do it myself on Honeymoon Day, that bungalow room, especially that bathroom, was going to be spotless, based on Centers for Disease Control standards, not the hotel's. I had already purchased our own bed linen, towels, and washcloths. I was going to purchase our own soap, toilet paper, and toiletries (I don't know what toiletries are, but women always say you need to get them)—and I was going to smuggle in a box of wet wipes, too!

Next to Old Harlem, there was Woodstock Falls. I landed on Graffiti Alley, which, despite its name, didn't have a speck of graffiti anywhere, ever. Woodstock Falls was a safe, working-class, multi-ethnic, but mostly Jewish, neighborhood. Like similar working-class neighborhoods, residents and business owners fiercely kept the trash—human and otherwise—away. The reason was simple—the residents didn't just work there; they lived there. The bottom half of the monolith skyscrapers was the businesses, and all above to the top was residential.

Good Kosher Market took up the entire length of the street, and that's saying a lot, since streets were ginormous in Metropolis. I never shopped anywhere else, because their food was natural—or, as I would say, "straight from the dirt." I avoided "processed" and felt the whole "organic" thing was nothing but a scam (by the unholy coupling of government and megacorps) to overcharge people for food. The Watts family had been serving nothing but quality food for more than a century. I had been a devoted customer and member of its select clientele for the last 12 years.

Good Kosher was my go-to market. It was where I always went, and would always go, until I was no longer alive. Like all its clientele, I knew every aisle, and every section. My shopping list was always made to match my path through the market with my hovercart. I knew all the staff by name, but the main staff were Mr. Watts and his sons. We, the clientele, were loyal to them, and they acknowledged that extreme loyalty every time we came, with nothing short of stellar customer service. It was a family business, where family actually worked the store, a rarity in Metropolis. There were no chains of Good Kosher, which we clientele always respected, because the specialness of the store would never be lost to the factory-like model of franchising. I was lucky to live close to Woodstock Falls, but clients came from the far ends of Metropolis to shop here and nowhere else. They had real food, not food masquerading as real, as in every other store, but no price gouging here either. Good Kosher was my market.

The store traffic was above normal today. I usually came at a different time of the day to avoid the rush-hour crowd, but I had to get my errands done. The cash register lines were long, but moving fast. What was great about Good Kosher was that, while they had the old-style cash register lines—no self-checkout here—they also had mobile cashiers who went down the lines, scanning and checking out clients with smaller loads to get them on their way.

But many times, regardless of how big your shopping load was, people preferred to wait in line, so they could get a chance to say hello to Mr. Watts and Sons. I was one of those clients, and told the mobile cashier to skip me, and help the person behind me.

Mr. Watts had to be in his late fifties, but there was nothing old about him. He had a full beard and mustache, with the hair graying at the temple and the edges of his beard. Like his sons, his uniform was a khaki jumpsuit with a fully-equipped utility belt, beaded strings around the neck, and a pointed Chinese bamboo hat to protect from the constant exposure of the artificial daylight ceiling lamps, which all Good Kosher's indoor natural plant life depended on.

"When do you leave?" Mr. Watts asked me.

"Tomorrow morning."

"You're going to have everything done by then, young man?"

"It will be done by tonight, even if I have to stay up all night."

"You'll be doing that tonight. Where will the wedding be?"

"The Bliss Resorts."

"Oh, nice. Fancy. The wife and I had ours at Eden Dawn. Bliss is very, very expensive."

"Tell me about it. I'll be paying the bills until I have white hair like you."

Mr. Watts grinned. "It's all worth it, young man. Well, as long as you don't get divorced. Otherwise, you have to do it all over again."

I pretended I wanted to faint.

"When you get back, come and see me."

"Sure. What do you need?"

"I'll have a case for you."

"A case?"

"Yes. Having a famous detective as a long-time client is an advantage I intend to use."

"It's not urgent?"

"No. Put it completely out of your mind. You're getting married."

"Can I leave my parents-in-law-to-be with you?"

"Young man, go. Embrace the end of bachelordom. Snuggle in the bosom of the horror that is one's parents-in-law."

"What if I paid you?" I asked.

CHAPTER 4

The Attorney

With the Pony loaded up with groceries, the next stop was home. Rabbit City was where I lived; it wasn't quite working-class, but it wasn't the dumps. My apartment tower was the Concrete Mama. It looked like a chunk of granite set down on Earth from space, and if there were ever a planetary shockwave from a nuclear blast or an asteroid crash, it would still be standing. It had been my home for 15 years.

I had a couple of hoverdolleys in the trunk of my vehicle, so I was able to efficiently load up the groceries on them, slowly pulling them from the lot to the elevators. For us lesser-tenants of the Concrete Mama, that lived on floors 100 and below, one had to go down to the ground-level main lobby and then use another set of elevators to go back up to your floor.

I came out into the main lobby, which, as usual, was filled with sidewalk johnnies hanging around, either coming from a street hustle, about to go out, or exchanging the day's gossip.

"Need help, Mr. Cruz?" the Concrete Mama's new doorman asked, with a Spanish accent.

Based on the nearly fatal consequences of hiring the building's first doorman, we were not about to make the same mistake twice. All the applicants had submitted to a full Metro and Federal background check first, and then the finalist would have to do an Up-Top check. All of this was at the applicant's expense, if they wanted the job.

The new doorman was a retired police officer, having served on Metro PD for 30 years working some of the toughest parts of the supercity. The second he'd applied, he was immediately at the top of the applicant pool, and it was no surprise when he was ultimately hired by the building's search committee.

He was Puerto Rican too, but unlike me, actually spoke Spanish. I was told he also spoke four other languages. We all liked the new doorman, and his presence classed up the place.

"I think I've got it, Mr. Post," I replied.

"Also, Mr. Cruz, your appointment has been waiting for about ten minutes."

"Oh, he's early."

I looked into the lobby again, and I saw the man in the suit seated on one of the lobby couches watching me.

This was big.

The future wife and I had decided we'd be living in the Concrete Mama, but my place was not big enough for her and me, and that was before any kids. We both needed extra space for home offices. Though I never expected to go back to the hovercar restoration biz ever again, I still wanted space for all my old hovercar stuff, and the room I had now also doubled as my personal weight room for exercising. As the famous fashionista that she was, Dot needed extra space for all her clothes, shoes, and accessories. I swear she had a different outfit for every day of the year.

My apartment was a legacy from my grandfather, and could be passed to children and descendants in perpetuity. Lady Luck had smiled on me. Last year, the building leaders of the Concrete Mama had wanted to get me out, after the chaos of my first major case, which is why they'd hired the first doorman to begin with. They'd changed their tune when they learned the doorman was a psycho crime boss, who was working on getting revenge on me, by blowing me—and the entire building—to bits. They'd made sure to include me in on the interviewing of all applicants and even asked me for recommendations, since I did know so many in law enforcement. It was at one of these interview meetings that I met the Manns. They lived in a Legacy apartment on the 150th floor, but in their advancing years, felt the space was too big for them to manage.

The real estate attorney was going to swap our legacies. A very complex legal process for laypeople, but not so for any busy legitimate real estate firm. It had to be done right, because the supercity would look for any loophole, to get their paws on your real estate property. He was from the same firm that had handled the paperwork and filings for my free Liquid Cool office space in Buzz Town.

First, we got the groceries to my place. Then we went up to the Mann's apartment complex, fifty levels up to sign all the paperwork.

"The Missus and I have been married 50 years," Mr. Mann said to me.

We were all seated at their kitchen table.

"Here, here, and here," the attorney directed them, as they continued to sign the paperwork.

"That's amazing. Dot and I will definitely try to get there too."

"When do you leave?" Mrs. Mann asked.

"Tomorrow."

"We're not delaying you, are we?" she asked.

"No, there's no hurry at all. Dot and I have the wedding and then the honeymoon. She still lives with her parents, but she has more stuff than I do. Next month is perfect for us. We'll move my things up, and your things down."

Mr. Mann looked around. "Yes, you two will love this place. It's much too much space for us now. We need smaller and simpler."

"You'll love my place, then."

I looked at the attorney, who was sitting quietly.

"All done?" I asked.

"We have everything I need for switching the residential legacy ownerships. I'll have the final documents ready for final signatures next month when you return, Mr. Cruz."

"Great. Another item to cross off the list."

"Mr. Cruz, a message from your secret benefactor: Congratulations on your wedding. Don't screw it up!"

CHAPTER 5

Pops

My secret benefactor?

The attorney purposely did that to get a rise out of me. I still had no idea who the person was who had given me unlimited use of the commercial space that was the offices of my Liquid Cool detective agency. It was the single stroke of luck that had helped usher in my new life as a private detective. Whoever he or she was, they were keeping abreast of my exploits.

I rushed back to my place to get a few quick house chores done, and then it was back in the Pony, to my next errand of my busy day. The TV was on in the living room, and there was my Pops, lounging on the recliner. He wasn't there when I had come in before, with the groceries.

"Pops, I thought you were gone already," I said.

"I was in the bathroom when you came in."

I was not going to expand that line of conversation further. I glanced at it, and was satisfied the door was open for maximum ventilation.

"I have more stops to make before going to the office."

"I have some errands to do, too. Let me borrow your car."

"Car?"

"Your vehicle. I have errands to do, too, and I don't want to call a hovercab. I can pick up your mother too. She's at the mall."

"But I have to go to my office."

"Cruz, I can drop you off at your office, do my errands, pick your mother up, and then pick you up from your office. Cruz, I was driving hovervehicles before you were born, and my vehicles were as fancy as yours, and I never put a dent in them, if that's what you're worried about."

All classic hovervehicle owners were the same. We didn't like other people driving our "babies." But what was I going to do? Pops was the father and a Kendo master, so I had to relent.

"Don't mess with my seat settings," I said, as I threw him the keys. "I have them just the way I like them. And we're leaving now, not at the end of whatever show you're watching."

He was laughing. "Kids. They always think the world only began when they were born."

"Well, yeah, I would consider that a true statement."

CHAPTER 6

Dog Man

Since I was going to be stranded without my own vehicle, I had Pops drop me off on the street near my office tower in Buzz Town. The rain wasn't coming down too hard, so I'd grab lunch.

Pops took the Pony about a foot off the ground to allow me to do a combat exit jump. I closed the door, and waved him off. I watched his driving form. Okay, my Pops knew how to drive. Oh, he taught me how to drive. I'd forgotten about that.

For a germophobe, I was surprisingly not concerned about getting my lunch from a local hoverfood truck. I blamed my associate, Phishy, for introducing this new thing into my routine. I rarely frequented restaurants and didn't normally do fast-food, or pizza delivery, but here I was at Dog Man's hoverfood truck.

This was his fifth food truck. He put the word out on the street that he was "the official hoverfood truck company frequented by Liquid Cool." At first, I wanted to sue the guy, but Phishy, my associate, did eat there, and had for years. He and Dog Man were friends. My wrath had been calmed, because his guerilla-street marketing campaign was not only increasing his business, but was sending a steady flow of business my way. Most were never going to be paying clients, but even if I got one legitimate client out of 50 contacts, then I considered it worth it.

"Mr. Cruz!" he yelled out when he saw me. A line of clients waiting for their hot dogs were staring at me. "People, this is the famous detective of Liquid Cool, himself, Mr. Cruz."

Now, there was excitement among the patrons as I stepped closer. I placed my money on his counter. "The usual, Dog Man."

"When do you get back from your wedding?" he asked me. "People, Mr. Cruz is getting married to the famous China Doll."

"I'll be back at work at the beginning of next month."

"Okay, I'll come see you then."

"What's going on?"

"Mr. Cruz, the Dog Man has a case for you." He handed me my change.

I hadn't even stepped into my work office yet, and I had two acquaintances wanting to hire me for cases. Cool!

CHAPTER 7

Flash

Since I didn't have my own vehicle, after I'd stuffed two rather delicious hot dogs into my face, and washed them down with some cherry cerveza, I walked to my building.

Buzz Town wasn't the best area, but it wasn't the worst—it was one of those in-between places, like Rabbit City, where I lived. Circuit Circle was a madhouse of pedestrian traffic. Slickers, neon umbrellas, colored shades, some visible cyborgs, a few on hoverskates—a typical crowd in the non-criminal part of the city.

I strolled into my 100th floor offices, and PJ's French music was playing. I didn't like any music I couldn't understand the words to, but as long as it kept her working—but no PJ.

Behind her reception desk was Flash.

Whenever I called Let It Ride Enterprises for mobile car security, he was the guy I called. Flash was a light-skinned Black guy, with a ponytail and a small goatee. He was always friendly, reliable, and took his job seriously, whether driving a hovercab or doing car-sitting security.

"Cruz," he greeted, wearing a yellow jumpsuit over his suit clothes.

"What? Flash, where's PJ?"

"She was called to the parking lot by the building. I was waiting, so she wanted me to sit at her desk."

"Flash, come out from behind there. The office will survive her not physically being at her desk for a moment. What were you waiting for?"

"Waiting for you."

"Me?"

"I want to hire you."

"Why does everyone want to hire me, today? I'm leaving for my wedding."

"I wanted to get on your calendar for when you get back. It'll keep 'til then."

"You're sure?"

"Positive. I'll wait for PJ to get back, and I'll see you tomorrow."

"You don't have to wait, Flash."

"It's fine."

"Hopefully, PJ won't be gone too long."

CHAPTER 8

Punch Judy

I sat at my desk in my private office, and scanned through the messages. PJ always printed them on memo sheets and stacked them according to priority—her priority. "Priority" meant they could pay to hire me. Second tier meant they could possibly pay. Third and last meant they were crazy, or wanted to talk to the famous detective—me, without disclosing their reasons.

I heard the door open, and commotion outside. I heard PJ's voice talking to Flash.

"See you tomorrow, Cruz!" Flash called out.

"Yeah, see you then!" I said.

I heard the front door close, and there was PJ.

Punch Judy.

My ex-felon secretary had short, dark crimson hair, and a simulated mole, a dot, above her lip—today was simple red lipstick day. When not in her big, black leather jacket, she liked to show off her bionic arms, so it was always sleeveless tops. This was the one with the Eiffel Tower on it, and she had on a shiny, studded silver belt over her black pants.

Friends called her Punch, girlfriends, Judy, everyone else, Punch Judy. She liked to punch people, and back when she was a posh-gang member, she could beat a person to a pulp. That was *before* she got the bionic arms. I called her PJ.

"There you are," I said to her. "Why did the parking lot call you?"

"Mr. Cruz, I was helping a client find the office." PJ was speaking in her professional voice. She only did that when she was with, or talking to, a confirmed wealthy client. PJ liked money, and so did I.

"A client?"

"Yes, Mr. Cruz. She's aware you will be out-of-town, but—"

"Out of town? You'll be out of town too. You're a bridesmaid."

"Mr. Cruz, the client is someone you have met before. She wants to wait for you, and have you work on her case exclusively—when you return."

"Who is this person I met before?"

I got up from my desk and walked into the reception-lobby.

Sitting there with shiny red lips, a clear red visor over her eyes, and her crossed black nylon legs, I saw the client I would simply call the Dame.

I had seen many beautiful women in my life. I was marrying one. This one was one of those movie star-model-politician trophy wife-cgi VR game bimbos—a description I would learn was quite prophetic. Later, I would know her by the name that everyone on the planet and beyond called her—NeuroDancer. I should have thrown her out of my office with her faux-British accent right there, but stupidly, I would take her case.

Had I known what was coming, I would have shot her then, but I didn't know. Besides, I had all my pre-wedding errands to finish.

PART TWO

The Movie-Town Metropolis Case

CHAPTER 9

China Doll

All the time I was growing up, I thought there was no one who had more family than my parents, and by extension, me. Of all the women in Metropolis, I had to marry the one woman on the planet who had more family than me.

"Where are all these people coming from?" I asked.

Seriously, people just kept coming into the temple. For every one person on my side of the family, three came in from her side of the family. I would've rather been water-boarded in slug-water; I so wanted this to be over.

The role of the groom was easy—just stand there. All kinds of people around you were doing stuff—the best man, the parents, the parents-in-law, the pastor. All you had to do was stand there and look cool. But how long could one do that? I knew Dot must have been saying the same thing in her top-secret bunker someplace in the temple: we should have eloped to New Vegas.

If all the adults weren't enough, there were kids everywhere. But at least, the munchkins got to run around, which was what I wanted to do—run, but take Dot with me. All the people in this temple constituted its own supercity.

"Where are all these people coming from?" I asked again, but I didn't expect any answer, only to be laughed at.

Finally, the end of the nightmare was at hand, when that creepy organ music began. Pops and Ma stood on my side, Run-Time, the best man was right behind me. Mrs. Wan was on the side for Dot. Then came the flower girls (Dot's nieces), the bridesmaids (Dot's sisters and PJ among them, showing off her buff bionic arms), with Mr. Wan leading Dot up the aisle, arms locked.

"We can still poison you." I turned to see my soon-, very soon-, to be mother-in-law leaning back after threatening me again, with a fake smile on her face.

They liked me now, because I was "famous."

I attempted to hypnotize myself and speed up time in my mind's eye. Walking up the aisle. Stopping. Pastor jabbering.

The only thing I cared about was Dot. She was known as China Doll, but women who knew her called her China; men called her Doll. Only her family and I called her by her real name—Dot. While I was "famous," she was really a famous style- and image-maker. When you saw her, she only wore the best clothes, with every piece of clothing, every accessory, and every piece of jewelry being the trendiest and the most stylish. Even today, confined to a white wedding dress, she had on a crystal necklace and matching crystal rings on each finger and a white neck scarf. She was always the fashionista to the very end, and her dress was truly one of a kind.

More pastor jabbering. Run-Time gave me the ring. I put the ring on Dot's finger.

"Hold on, young man," the pastor said. "Simon didn't say to put that ring on her finger yet."

"Oh," I said, and took the ring off.

There were too many people in this temple, because when they started laughing, it was like a NASCAR-Fujiyama hovercar race stadium audience laughing, the sound echoing through the space, almost picking you off the ground.

"Young man, now you can place the ring on her finger." He looked at the others. "The groom's ring."

Dot yelled something in Chinese at her father, and he fished it out of his pocket, embarrassed. He handed it to her. She placed the ring on my finger.

"Okay, young people, are we ready for the end?"

"Yes, please," I said. My voice from the microphone sounded as if I were yelling, and got the wedding crowd laughing again.

"Young people nowadays have no patience."

The end was at hand. I blanked out all the irrelevant parts.

"I do," I said.

"I do," Dot said.

"I now pronounce you husband and wife."

Finally! I kissed my wife to everyone's cheers. We got hugs. Run-Time patted me on the back.

"Now, we can dance all night long!" my Pops yelled to the crowd, and they all yelled back, "Yeah!"

"Just shoot me now," I said. The day was never going to end.

Dot gave me another kiss.

CHAPTER 10

The Man From the Studio

Almost 18 months of planning, rehearsals, burning through money and—it was over—finally. Wedding, honeymoon, and moving into our new Concrete Mama apartment was done.

I was blazing my way in the Pony to my Liquid Cool office, with my driving gloves on, gripping the wheel. It was time to go to work and earn some cash. That's what famous private detectives do, especially ones with a wife now.

The one thing I had to give to my cyborg secretary, PJ, was that she loved to continuously add to the ambience of the office. I wasn't sure if it was a French thing; the word was. She was always clipping articles from the newsfeed about me to hang up on the Liquid Cool walls. Clients did love reading them, while they waited in the lobby. It was a great conversation starter, and PJ was the office tour guide down Liquid Cool's expanding memory lane.

When I got in, all I had to do was waltz into my private office, press the button on the coffee maker (a wedding gift), plant my butt in the chair, and be ready for my first appointment for my first day back post-honeymoon. Since PJ set it up, they would be a genuine paying client, and she would have already gotten the "preliminary retainer." It was easy enough to refund, if they turned out to be bat-crazy, or a case I wasn't interested in.

PJ spent a lot of time with the client in the yellowish suit pointing out some of Liquid Cool's best moments in the media, which she had some kind of picture representation of on the wall. By the time she showed him into my private office, the man was still smiling, upon meeting me.

"A real life private detective," he said, shaking my hand vigorously. "Like in the movies. Ever thought of having a movie or TV series, fictional or reality, of your cases?"

"Maybe, when I'm old, gray and need extra retirement money."

I directed him to sit.

"Why wait until the deadly years, Mr. Cruz? Never put off being filthy rich tomorrow when you can do it today, my boss always says."

"I can't disagree with that. What can I do for you, Mr. Branch?"

"How's your schedule tomorrow? Would after lunch work for you?"

"After lunch work for what?"

"To come out to the studios to meet my boss. He's the one who wants to retain your services."

"Not you?"

"Oh, no. I'm only the boot-licking, sycophant assistant, who gets an associate producer credit every now and again. They send me to check things out. Mr. Meta is a very busy man. We're on deadline, so he can't leave the studios, but we can have the famous detective go to him. Mr. Meta will be tickled to meet a real live private eye working the mean streets of Metropolis—and he wears a vintage fedora! Priceless. You're right out of a script for the next crime thriller blockbuster."

"I'm flattered, Mr. Branch—but wouldn't a major movie studio have its own private investigation firm on retainer?"

"We have several, Mr. Cruz, but I'll have Mr. Meta explain the situation. We have to go—off-the-books on this one."

"I understand."

"Excellent. Shall I send over the studio hoverlimo at, say—12:30?"

CHAPTER 11

The Movie Mogul

I had been hired by all types of private citizens, government officials, and corporates, but never an actual movie studio. I had no idea what to expect. All I had to go with was all the stereotypes of what Movie-Town was like, no different from any other citizen of Metropolis.

Branch's shiny silver hoverlimo arrived at 12:30 pm at my Liquid Cool office the next day. One of the chauffeurs opened the door for me, though he didn't have to, but customer service is customer service.

Body Shot Studios was in Opus Fields, a wealthy section of the supercity near Silicon Dunes, Silver City and not far from Elysian Heights where my parents-in-law lived. Opus Fields was Movie-Town. There were monolith towers like any other part of the supercity, but most of it was open space, where robots were constantly changing the landscape for one movie set or another—whether an Ancient Western, dinosaur-infested prehistoric jungle, or outer galactic volcanic world. I saw all those environments, and many more.

As the hoverlimo coasted into the studio headquarters tower, I saw there was probably more security here than even City One, or Police

One. In the real world, studio heads and movie stars did get more security than the Mayor, City Council, or the Police Chief.

Branch was waiting for me, and he led me to an awaiting hovercart. As we drove across the lot, he pointed out the sites to me, as if his duties also included being a tour guide.

"Actually, that's how I began my career at the studios," he said. "I was a tour guide first. I got my big break when a kid threw up on me, and he turned out to be one of the producer's kids. The rest, as they say, is history."

I always thought my best friend's office—Run-Time, CEO of Let It Ride Enterprises—was humongous. I had thought the Mayor's office was humongous. I had seen offices of royal families, like the Royal Lux, and of megacorp executives, like Mr. Yo at Orochi Corp, and thought they were humongous. All those offices were tiny video-phone booths, compared to the office of Mr. Meta. When Branch led me into the office, I thought I was in an air-space terminal, it was so big.

In a corner of the "room" far, far, far away, I saw the figure of a standing man, waving his hands all around. As we came closer, I could begin to make out what he was saying.

"He's going to be an archaeologist, who teaches history classes to hot babes by day, and during the school breaks, treks around the planet recovering supernatural artifacts with cyborg Nazis on his heels. Yes, his primary weapon is this laser whip! How are you with the short list for the love interest?"

"Mr. Meta," Branch interrupted.

The man noticed us. "Ah, gentlemen, let's continue this later tonight."

There were four other men in suits seated. They all stood, gathering mobile computers.

"Great concept, sir," one of them said.

Each of them said something similar as they headed out of the room, and Branch directed me to his boss.

"Mr. Cruz," he said, as he took my hand, and started shaking it so hard, I thought he'd shake it right out of the socket. "I've heard so many amazing things about you. Branch, get this man a drink! What'll you have? You name it."

"A cup of silk coffee is fine."

"Branch, a dirty martini for me."

"Oh, it's one of those kinds of meetings. Change mine to a Japanese whiskey, then."

"Much better," Mr. Meta said. "Sit, Mr. Cruz, sit."

Branch disappeared, and Meta and I sat.

"How long have you been a detective, Mr. Cruz?"

"Not even two years yet."

"Amazing—and you've already made a name for yourself. I heard about you for the first time last year, when the criminals were trying to take over Metropolis. City Hall and Up-Top, versus the entire Metro Police Department. It was like the supercity version of World War TV. I saw you then, Mr. Cruz. You were the one who lit the fuse, but you were the one who saved it. I said to my people then, 'That Cruz, he's an up-and-comer. Keep an eye on him. One day, we'll have to sign him to a reality TV contract. Mark my words.'"

"I'm flattered."

"I'm not saying it to flatter you, Mr. Cruz. I'm saying it to plant the seed so that, one day, we can make a space-boat-full of money."

I laughed. Branch returned with our drinks. I sipped mine, but Mr. Meta gulped his down. Branch disappeared again, to continue his drink duties.

"What can I do for you, Mr. Meta? Your associate said it was a matter that couldn't be handed over to your normal private investigation firms."

"Normal isn't the word I'd use to describe them. Bastards and quasi-criminals, the lot of them. But that's what you need in the movie business. No, I can't go to them, because I don't trust them. I trust them to do studio business, but not to do my business."

"How can I help?"

Branch returned with another glass for him, and Mr. Meta leaned back in his chair. "Mr. Cruz, I believe you can help me." He gulped down the alcohol, and handed it to Branch again. "Blackmail."

Branch was gone again. "How long?" I asked.

"Years, Mr. Cruz."

"You've been paying them all this time?"

"Yes."

"Why?"

"It was easier."

"What has changed?"

"They want more money. Substantially more money. I realize it's never going to end."

"What do you want me to do, then?"

"Mr. Cruz, I want you to find something for me to blackmail him with."

It wasn't my first blackmail case, but in those cases, the client had me make the payments for them, explain to the blackmailer that there would be no further payments, but blackmailing the blackmailer was new.

"Is the blackmailer a criminal?"

Mr. Meta laughed. "Of course."

"I want to be clear on what you'd consider a successful outcome on this case. You want me to find something to blackmail the blackmailer, to use as leverage, so that he doesn't increase the blackmail payments ever again, but you'll continue to pay the blackmail payments—and you don't want me to ask why you'll continue to make those blackmail payments."

"Mr. Cruz, you should consider a career in script coverage. That's it, exactly."

"I'll poke around for a couple of days. Not every criminal has something to blackmail them with, or even cares."

"Mr. Cruz, I'm surprised you haven't made any moral arguments, or tried to get me to go to the police."

"Mr. Meta, I'm a big boy. I know others have already done that, and you've already had those discussions with yourself. You've decided not to, so I won't waste the time of either of us."

"You're not even going to try to ask me what he's blackmailing me about."

"Mr. Meta, if you want to tell me, okay, but I really don't care. All I need is the information on the blackmailer, and I'll take it from there."

Branch returned to hand Mr. Meta another drink, but the studio chief didn't gulp it down this time.

"Branch," Mr. Mogul said. "I never thought it possible, but I think we've found the perfect detective."

CHAPTER 12

Beat Box

I was highly motivated in the case. The movie business was all about who you knew. A good recommendation by one could lead to an avalanche of business. If it were not for that, I wouldn't have taken the case. Blackmail, domestic violence, cheating spouses, they were all grimy, slimy cases that I wanted to elevate Liquid Cool above and beyond. Not that every case had to be the Watch Conspiracy, or Blade Gunner, but they didn't have to be me crawling around with the low-lifes of Metropolis either. I wanted the clean middle ground.

That was the theory, anyway.

Branch gave me a file so thick, on a street hustler named Beat Box, that it was heavy enough for me to break a sweat doing bicep curls. It was clear from the file that Mr. Meta had used his studio private investigation firms to compile deep-background intel on the criminal. I was hired to take it to the next step.

The Body Shot studio hoverlimo dropped me back at my Liquid Cool office, and I spent the balance of the day reviewing it. I had read lots of police files, but when corporate investigators of a megacorp studio investigated a person, the thoroughness was always taken to a much deeper level. I knew so much about Beat Box that I could impersonate him—except for a few things.

Again, I was in the seedy Whiskey Way. My first major case was hatched in this place, and it was next to another seedy town, Mad Heights (or Mad City), where if I never ever set foot there in my entire life, that wouldn't be long enough.

The good parts of Metropolis had sidewalk johnnies and sallies—harmless, low-level street hustlers that worked the streets. The bad areas had the dope daddies, dope fiends, fast-finger freddies, graffiti bandits, cyberpunks, and assorted street gangs. When you visited the mean streets of Metropolis, you'd better know what you were getting yourself into.

Fifty percent of the supercity were cyborgs. Before becoming a detective, I only came across them every so often. Since becoming a detective, I had seen more of them than I cared for. It seemed there was an over-representation of them in the criminal world. Despite that, I was always the one who said not all cyborgs were criminals. My ex-felon, cyborg secretary always took the "most cyborgs are criminals" stance. I didn't care what was the correct stance. I just didn't want to get shot, whether by a cyborg skell or non-cyborg one.

As I walked through the BarFly Bar, my eyes scanned the premises. The lights were so dim, and there was so much drug smoke in the place, I could barely see anything. I was wearing my air regulator mask over my mouth and clear goggles over my eyes to keep me drug-free before, during, and after entering the nasty place to find my "buddy," Beat Box.

I was at the bar and about to order a drink for show, when the bartender leaned to me and asked, "Are you a narc?"

"Why do you think I'm a narc?"

"You're the only one in the place with a mask on."

"I'm particular about inhaling foreign substances when I don't know what they are, and who they're from. I just got married, and I'd like to make sure my first born doesn't pop out with three arms, or a big eye in the center of his forehead."

The bartender started to laugh. "Okay, you got a legit point there. There are some foul drugs in the air in here."

"Give me a glass of your most expensive booze, and point to where that bum Beat Box is. I know he's here."

"Owes you money?"

"That's why I ordered your most expensive drink, because I'm going to pay for it, and he's going to reimburse me, and give me everything else he owes me. Why do you let that free-loading bum into your classy joint?"

The bartender placed my order in front of me. "Have you ever seen Beat Box in person?"

"I have a secret to tell you."

The bartender leaned forward. "What?"

"Beat Box isn't a seven-foot-Russian-looking cyborg psycho. He's a three-foot Black midget hiding in an android suit."

The bartender started laughing. "You're lying."

"You want to bet?"

"I'll bet the price of your drink. You're lying. Everybody knows Beat Box. He's been terrorizing these streets for ages. If that were true, someone on the street would have let that slip."

"He's hated that much?"

"He's hated, all right."

Another bartender appeared next to us. "If that were true, we'd take him out."

"I'm going to prove it right now. Where is that bum?"

The two bartenders pointed to the upstairs level in unison.

High-stakes neon pool was the game. Every kind of criminal had their big butts planted on stools, watching four different matches going on at the same time. Standing everywhere, with drinks and butts in hand, were bar spectators—lots of skin showing, and glowing clothes and hair. One of the matches was the rock-hard, crew-cut, mean-looking Beat Box.

"I am going to win the game of the day, like I do every night, and take all you hairy-fairies' money!" he declared in a Russian accent, raising his giant arm in the air, holding his red-lit cue stick. "Why? Because I'm great, and you're not, suckers!"

"Hey, Beat Box!" I yelled.

The thug turned to me. If I had drawn on him, he would have shot me down. Many others had made that mistake before. I simply threw a blue magnetic pellet at the side of his head. It attached, and his entire body started vibrating violently. It stopped, his eyes pulled back into their sockets, and suddenly, Beat Box's body started to open. It was a machine suit, and out fell the real Beat Box—a three-foot Black midget!

Everyone's mouth hung open in disbelief, except for mine. The Beat Box sat on the floor like a little toddler, with his mouth hanging open, too. Everyone looked at him. He stared back. Everyone's faces turned to snarls and clenched teeth. The real Beat Box's face turned to sheer terror.

Suddenly, the android suit fell back and crashed to the ground behind him.

"Get him!" someone yelled.

The real Beat Box scurried under one of the pool tables, like a frightened mouse. People dived after him.

The beating was savage. It was the entire second floor, joined by the first floor, including all the wait staff, including the two bartenders. If I hadn't dragged him out of there, he would have been stomped to death. If he were a murderer, rapist, or pedophile, I would have left him to meet his end. He was a very bad guy, but his sadism didn't extend past viciously beating up other criminals for fun. He was a bone-breaker and enforcer, who cheated at cards.

I didn't like strangers in my Pony, but here I was driving the black, blue, and bloodied Beat Box—the real one—to Metro General.

"Let's be very clear about this situation, Mr. Beat Box. If I hadn't pulled you out of there when I did, you'd be so many levels of dead that there wouldn't have been enough DNA for CSI to gather up for the RIP box. You hearing me?"

"What—what do you want?"

"I am in the employ of a Mr. Meta."

"Oh, God. Don't take me to him, please. I'll pay you not to take me to him."

"I think he has far more money than you."

"But the money I have is far more than you have. I'll give it to you, and you let me go."

"Mr. Beat Box, this is what we're going to do. Since your days on the street are over, I'm going to get Mr. Meta to make a lump sum and final blackmail payment to you. What will you do when you receive that payment?"

"Disappear, and never contact him again."

"You do understand me. I'm going to dump you at Metro General to clean up your sorry carcass, and I'm not going to ask you what you feel is a 'fair' final lump sum blackmail payment. Whatever, and I do mean whatever, he says is fair will be fair as far as you're concerned. You'll receive the money, and you turn over all the blackmail material, whatever it is, and that will conclude our business. Do you have any objections, Mr. Beat Box? There's still time for me to turn my vehicle around, and dump you back at the bar."

"You're the one in the driver's seat. When you're not sitting in the driver's seat, you can't object to anything at all. I also notice your vehicle has one of those illegal passenger eject features."

"Only a criminal would know what that button does, Mr. Beat Box."

The button was a fake, of course—but he didn't know that.

"I don't know who you are, but you know how to negotiate. Since I can't fly, and have no desire to return to the bar, your deal is accepted with the sincerest enthusiasm I can muster in my beaten condition."

CHAPTER 13

Mr. Meta

PJ couldn't patch in the video-call fast enough.

"Mr. Cruz!" Mr. Meta was beaming from the screen. "Under-promise, over-deliver! That's how you do it! You wrapped this case up quickly, quietly, and with textbook finesse. No blackmail. No blackmailer. I don't know how you did it, Mr. Cruz, but I don't care. It's done. You are a true professional, who knows his craft, and Mr. Branch is on his way to your offices with a healthy bonus."

If I'd been wondering whether if PJ was listening in on my video-calls from her desk, I knew for sure now. She was dancing.

CHAPTER 14

Mr. Caret

I knew I was going to be getting new business from movie types. I didn't know I'd get a call the very next day. Once again, a hoverlimo picked me up from my Liquid Cool office. Do all these movie guys have their own limo services?

This time, the destination wasn't to a studio, but a card joint in Star Town—another upscale part of the supercity. It was an upscale establishment, where everything on the menu was expensive, even the ice in your glass of alcohol. It was also a go-to place for Movie-Town types who loved their card games.

"Who's this?" The man at the bar seemed as if he were waiting for us.

"Get lost," my thug escort said to the man, but was ignored.

"I know," the man said to me, smiling. "The name's Beta Max." He pointed to me. "We'll connect one of these days." The man got up from his stool and left.

"Who is that guy?" I asked.

"Forget him," my thug escort replied. "Beta Max is nobody."

Yes, I did intend to forget him. But, no, I didn't think he was nobody. He looked familiar to me, too. I just couldn't place him.

"Jokers, boys! When the jokers are wild, I get wild. Wild and crazy. Give me them jokers, so I can take your money!"

Mr. Caret was the potential client, who'd sent the hoverlimo. He was the center of attention in the room, with all kinds of suits with glasses of booze in one hand, smokes in the other, around him. Caret's table had a huge pot in the center, and even from where I was standing, with the thug-in-a-suit Caret had sent to fetch me in the hoverlimo, everyone at the table was sweating badly.

"Who needs Lady Luck, when you've got Joker's luck?" Caret said, half-laughing, and threw his cards down.

We could all hear some of Caret's card-mates swallow their own tongues.

"That, boys, is how it's done, joker-style," Caret said and grabbed all that money from the center of the table to pull to him. "I *luv* me some money."

No movie had the outlandish characters I was running into in this case.

Caret's man took me to some back offices. One of them was where Caret eventually made his way, and grabbed my hand.

"Mr. Cruz, it's a pleasure to meet the private eye," he said. "You come highly recommended."

His man directed me to sit. Caret pulled his chair closer to mine, and when he sat, he wasn't just next to me. He might as well have been sitting on my lap.

"When you come highly recommended in this town, Mr. Cruz, that means you saved someone enough money to fill an asteroid, kept them out of jail, or kept their dirty laundry out of the press. Mr. Cruz, I need all three! Full service package, please."

"How can I help?"

Caret shrunk back into his chair. "I'll paint the picture for you.

"I didn't know my father for a long time. The man I called 'father' for most of my pre-adult life was not. Meeting my real father was quite a traumatic event. I wanted to kill him. He wanted to kill me. All the usual plot points.

"In the end, we patched things up, said nice things to each other, and I thought we were good. You know how things go. One minute you're the scariest, badass in the universe. Next, they may remember your name, but don't know who you are. Some new guy comes along and replaces you. So you have to fill that void. Bring meaning to your life again. You find—wait for it—spirituality."

Mr. Caret was a business-man-turned-movie producer. That was the nice way of saying it for public consumption. The real deal was, he was an ex-gangster, with a flair for the melodramatic, who now fancied himself a big moviemaker. He would never win any awards for his high-action, heavily-titillating fare, but his movies were making lots of money. In Movie-Town, that was the only bottom line that mattered.

"My father is being used by a cult; that's what I call it, what he's a member of. They believe there's a force that permeates all living things, and the entire universe. This force elevates all its learners to a plane of higher consciousness. The next level in this force, learners become 'knights' and hand over all their earthly possessions to the Master.

"You can see where I'm going with this, Mr. Cruz. These cult people are stealing my father's money, so their Master can fatten his own bank account and surround himself with drugs and prostitutes. He can do all of that, but not with my father. Not with his money, my money, either."

"What do you want me to do?" I asked.

"Get my father out of there."

"Okay—"

Caret raised a finger, while he shook his head. "I know what you're thinking, Mr. Cruz. You're thinking this is easy-peasy. You think you go in, snatch him up, and deliver him to me. Mr. Cruz, I'm warning you now, this may be the most dangerous case you've ever tangled with, and you are about to do battle with the most ruthless, dastardly evil-doers you've ever come across. They could practically crush your neck with a mere look."

"These evil-doers are who exactly?"

"All of them. It's a big cabal of them."

"What's the name of this cult?"

"The House of the Jed."

"Jed?"

"That's their Master, and one other thing you should know, Mr. Cruz."

"What would that be?"

"My father...suffers from...delusions. He thinks—he is the greatest villain in the universe. He *may* be clinically psychotic. Maybe a smidgen sociopathic. He could potentially, now I say potentially, not probably, try to kill you—but just think of him as my good 'ol father."

CHAPTER 15

NeuroDancer

I sat there trying to come up with the best way to say, "Hell no. I'm not taking this case."

"Mr. Cruz."

I immediately recognized the sultry, mesmerizing voice of that last client of the day before I flew away to become a married man.

"Nova," I heard Caret say, as he stood from his chair and ran to her.

He planted a kiss on her cheek. They held hands as they approached me.

"Skybaby, how could you tell Mr. Cruz a story like that? He must be thinking the worst."

"He's a trooper. There's no storm he can't weather," Caret said.

"Mr. Cruz, it is not nearly as dangerous as my squeeze would have you believe. Look into it for a few days for us. Decide then if you can commit to the case."

"That seems fair," I said.

"You've never seen her," Caret said to me, smiling.

"I actually have—"

"No. You've never seen a NeuroDancer show."

"I can't say that I have."

Caret looked at his man. "You will."

"Don't be rude, Skybaby," she said to him. "Mr. Cruz is a busy man. Take him home, so he can look into your case for you."

"Yes," Caret said and looked at his men. "Take Mr. Cruz home. Mr. Cruz, it was a pleasure meeting you in person. If there's any private detective in this city who can resolve my case, it's you."

"If I do decide to take the case, based on what you said about your father, bringing him home to you wouldn't be the best thing, would it?"

Caret began laughing hysterically. "Bring him to me? No, Mr. Cruz. When he's rescued, I'm having him locked up in the Metro Insane Asylum. Then I can finally get all his money."

CHAPTER 16

Rogue One

That was nice of Caret to admit. His issue wasn't that the "cult," as he called it, was going to get his father's money. It was that they'd get it before he could.

When Caret's thug-in-a-suit dropped me back at my Liquid Cool office, I noticed a man on the street for a second. The first time I'd seen him was when we were in Caret's card joint. Now, that man was on the same street I was on, following me. I had decided to take a scenic route around the building, rather than march up to my offices.

If he were any good, he'd know I was leading him into an ambush. Well, he wasn't any good—an amateur. He wasn't even good enough to blend into the crowds. My walking got faster, the crowds got bigger, and the rain had started down a bit heavier. I decided to take him as soon as I turned the next corner.

Rat-tat-tat!

I knew the sound of practically every weapon there was to hear on Earth. It was machine-gun fire, and my amateur tail was spraying everyone in my vicinity to get me. I saw people run, try to run, or collapse to the ground in the hail of bullets.

This wasn't a matter of protecting myself. It was a matter of killing the guy before he could kill or shoot any more innocent people. Every millisecond I delayed meant another man, woman, or child unlucky enough to be near me at this given time and place could be killed.

He was an amateur. I wasn't. Every shot from my omega-gun hit him. All I wanted to hear was the end of the machine-gun fire from his weapon. I got what I wanted as he fell to the ground.

PART THREE

The Man of the Galaxy Case

CHAPTER 17

Officers Bus and Boot

I called them "sucker shooters." They'd try to ambush you and shoot you in the back. When I first started as a detective, I came across quite a few of them. They all missed, and one, I shot out of my 100-story Liquid Cool office window.

This was different. I wasn't alone. This crazy maniac sprayed a crowd of innocent people on the street to get me. It was truly a miracle of all miracles that no one was killed. Plenty of people were shot, but it was nothing the hospital couldn't fix. However, children were involved, and that wouldn't be so easy to "fix." More than anything else, I knew that letting loose on my sucker shooter saved lives. It was not about bravado, or being some kind of galactic James Bond-style agent.

I knew the routine. Sit quietly on the pavement as the police did their thing. This time, however, there were no "Ebony and Ivory"—my favorite police "buddies," who were often the ones to respond to any call that involved me. I was told there was even a special police code that was created to refer to me.

"Where's Officers Break and Caps?" I asked the duty officers.

"Vacation," Office Boot answered.

Metro police wore visored half-helmet and silver-and-black body-armored uniforms with PEACE in big bold white letters on their chests, but they could kill you in an instant, if you did the wrong thing. Officer Boot was the bigger Russian one, and Officer Bus was the Italian one.

"Cruz, can you explain to us why you're always shooting someone dead or someone is trying to shoot you dead?"

"I don't know who the guy is."

"Was," Officer Bus corrected.

"Was. I saw him following me. I led him away from my office, and was going to confront him when I turned the corner. I had no idea he was packing. I've never seen him before."

"What cases are you working on?"

"None that would lead to this guy trying to kill me. Who is he? I've never seen him before."

"Cruz, we need you to come down to Central."

"Not again." I threw my hands up in the air. "He shot at me."

"Cruz, he's going down to Central, and you're going down to Central. Did you really think you'd shoot someone dead in the middle of the street and we'd just say 'Oh, Cruz, it's all handled. We'll catch you later?'"

"No, I guess not. But I had to try."

How long was I at Metro Central, a.k.a. Police One, a.k.a. Metro PD, a.k.a Central? Five hours! My whole day was shot. I could have gotten out of there after three and a half hours, but I was determined to get all the details on the man who tried to kill me.

I finally got a peek at the file, and couldn't get out of there fast enough. I was lucky, because the Police Chief was also on vacation. Had he been there, I would have been there another five hours.

Needless to say, PJ had gone home, and the building's night staff was on duty when I finally strolled into my office. My office had great security now, but I still didn't like to be there after hours. There were 24-hour buildings, and those like mine, that were strictly day buildings. It was packed during day hours, but afterward, it was a ghost town. Day hours in a supercity where it always rained. Day and night looked like the same thing, but there was still a day and night. At night, the only place I wanted to be was home.

I sat at my desk in my private office. I flipped through the file they gave me of the rogue who'd tried to shoot me dead. I looked at the name, but it might as well have been John Doe. I didn't know him. Never met him. He had no criminal record and, unlike me as of recently, didn't even have a ticket from a traffic cop. What was clear to me was that this guy had never held a machine-gun, or any gun, ever in his life. He hadn't accounted for the kick, and most of his machine-gun spray went above all of us. It could have been disastrous if he had been a professional. I wouldn't be confronting anyone else without my weapon already drawn ever again.

One factoid screamed out at me as soon as I saw it. He was an accountant at one of the Movie-Town studios.

Why would a movie studio accountant try to kill me?

Did I just step into something with my last Movie-Town case, or was it for something I was about to step into? An accountant tried to kill me. I had thought accountants were nice, non-violent people.

CHAPTER 18

Logo

I eventually did get home. I didn't want to wake Dot, so I slept on her bean bag couch, which I absolutely loved, which had replaced my previous non-bed sleeping place—the couch. That was boring. Dot's bean bag sucked you in, and I swear you dozed off in a matter of minutes.

Four a.m. was when I got home, and I had to be back at the office at no later than 8 a.m., so I wasn't even going to see her before she was up to get ready for work. My goal was at least to stop by her work so we could have lunch.

I had beaten PJ to the office, which impressed her. "You better be in the office early," she said. "I heard you shot someone again."

I told PJ what had really happened. All she cared about was that I hadn't gotten myself arrested, and that I was in the office to meet more clients.

"I got a good new client for you," she announced. "He's Japanese, too, so I'll have some Japanese stuff around. That's what I'll be doing in my new role of chief client concierge manager."

"What?"

"I anticipate the psychosocial needs of premium clients," she continued. "Add familiarity to the Liquid Cool office, to encourage strong relationships. Strong relationships lead to the higher likelihood of bonuses from satisfied clients."

"PJ, I don't know what you just said, but if you're happy, and it doesn't cost me any money, then there will be no complaints from me."

He was one smooth customer. He arrived 15 minutes early, and he and PJ spent the time talking about some joint French-Japanese space cruiser of the past.

When he got to my office, he didn't do that Japanese bow thing that I could never do. He shook my hand, looked around my office, and sat down.

"Mr. Cruz, I am happy to make your acquaintance."

"Thank you, Mr. Logo. How can I help?"

"In my line of work, we hire many private detectives, but they are always the ones who occupy the lower rungs of the profession."

"What line of work are you in, Mr. Logo?"

"Opposition research. Politics."

"Deep background? People or companies?"

"Both, and other related duties. I must say it will be an honor to work with a higher breed of private detective."

"I hope I can live up to my reputation."

He reached over from his chair, and handed me a card. "This man will be calling you tomorrow."

I took the card, and immediately recognized his name.

"Good, you know him."

"What do they call him?"

"The Man of the Galaxy."

"We use that term 'galaxy' so much, when we only inhabit one small part of a solar system."

"We must always live as though we can go beyond the stars," Logo said with a smile.

"Is he a client?"

"An adversary."

"What are you here to hire me to do, then?"

"I'm hiring you to take his case, no matter what it might be."

"Mr. Logo, I don't quite understand."

"You will at the proper time. It's important for my company that he gets the help he seeks."

"Your adversary?"

"In my business, today's adversary is tomorrow's client. He will, of course, lose his election bid. Based on the election cycle, he'll then look to hire a better company the next time around, pay whatever is required."

I sat there with a smirk. What a crafty weasel he was.

"You have it all planned."

"But of course."

"I'm trying to think of any ethical issues there might be, but can't come up with any. What if he has a case I can't handle?"

"It will not be outside the scope of your usual cases. Besides, I'm paying you to take his case."

"An extra pay day for me today means a much bigger pay day for you in the future."

"Think of it as a business partnership." He smiled. "How about I throw in a couple of tickets for you and the new wife to see a live show?"

CHAPTER 19

The Politician

The three men were the most fidgety people I had ever met.

PJ brought them into my office for their appointment.

"How often do you sweep for listening devices?" one of them asked, looking around.

"What about video surveillance devices?" another asked.

"There are neither in this office, here in my private office, or in the general area outside. We sweep weekly," I said.

"Not daily?"

"No, not daily, Mr. Paranoid. Why don't we meet at his house instead?"

"That would not be wise at all. You are known to the public. Someone would certainly recognize you."

"Gentlemen, see my secretary on the way out. You can call her to set up whatever off-site meeting you'd like, but you will pay me for my travel and time."

The men were not happy with my instructions.

"Good day, gentlemen."

They slowly stood from their chairs, and shuffled out the door.

"Sorry, Mr. Cruz, for our behavior," one man said. "We don't mean to be overly paranoid. The problem is that we've had plenty of reasons to be paranoid. Hope you never get to the place we're at."

After the men left, I found myself looking around my office.

PJ was at my office doorway.

"Don't listen to those stupid people. Liquid Cool offices have no bugs at all."

"Remember my last case? Bugs set up my place. After that, I found those snakes in my shower. Let's make sure."

Bugs was the best electronics sweeper and security gadget man in the business.

Another hoverlimo ride. This time, it was to Silver City, which, based on my last case, was not a place I was eager to return to either. I didn't even know there were any residential towers in Silver City. There was—taller than most in Metropolis. This was where the Man of the Galaxy lived.

The three men were there, clearly more relaxed in their secure environment.

"Let us have the room," Mr. Cruces said as he entered.

The three men left, and he sat across from me, after he'd shaken my hand. "Mr. Cruz."

"Mr. Cruces."

"I'm not one to bring strangers into my affairs, but everyone whose opinions I trust all say the same thing about you: You know how to work discreetly, and know how to keep secrets for the greater good. I need your help in disposing of a problem."

"What problem would that be?" I asked.

"I have an extended family member that I don't want anyone to know about."

"You're running for Federal office, and you have some illegitimate children out there that you want out of reach from your political adversaries? Because it would damage your squeaky image, Man of the Galaxy image?"

"Very good, Mr. Cruz. I like a man who can cut right to the heart of things. I wish I had advisers who could do the same. It's so tedious dealing with them most times. Are you able to help me with my problems?"

"I can."

He watched me for a moment. "No questions?"

I shook my head. "No. I'm sure you have all the files I need and full payment. I'll get working right away."

"I have everything ready for you in the next room. I can't let you take the files, but you can take notes in whatever cryptic fashion you can make up and remember. As for money, that is simply a video-call away. Payments will be spread out over each completed task."

"I'll start now."

He led me to another room, where those three aides were waiting. Mr. Cruces said his goodbyes, and left me with them. They watched me closely as I read the files. Man of the Galaxy. The sleazy horn-dog. He had 20 kids all over the place, separate from his wife and legitimate six kids. Most of his money must have been going to keeping the mothers quiet, and providing for his army of children.

However, in the detective business, you can't be overly choosy about your clientele, or you'd find yourself with no clients. High tech world, low-life people.

CHAPTER 20

The House of Jed

I did still have Mr. Caret's case to resolve.

The House of Jed was marked by a large humanoid statue with its arms raised to the sky and palms upward. Beaming out into the heavens from those palms was a powerful ray of light. When I flew into Asphalt Park in my Pony that was what I locked in on, because the actual temple was underground. This part of Metropolis didn't seem like a town at all. There was the temple in the center of a giant concrete park. The large avant-garde "park" had trees, bushes, and benches all made of concrete. Who would hang out there in the rain? Not even sidewalk johnnies came to the place, so it remained empty. Taxpayer money at work for nonsense. But for the temple people, it was perfect.

I was not sure what I felt about a religious group whose temple was underground, eye-level with vermin, and even creepier, for me, was entering the main door, which was carved out of their statue's big toe. Vermin and toe fungus, that's what was in my mind as I came through the door.

The two who greeted me were wearing hooded white robes.

"Good morning, brother. Are you here to learn more about the force of the universe?" one asked.

I presented them with a photo of Caret's father. "Hey, brother," I began, "could you help a brother out, and take me to this brother?"

The two disciples looked at the photo and removed their hoods.

"No, brother," the female one said, "but we can take you to our leader."

Was she mocking me? I couldn't tell, but they led me into the elevators; down we went. We were going down fast, and I didn't like it at all. The thought did cross my mind that we were going to pop out at the other side of the planet, we were descending so far.

The elevators opened, and there weren't one, but three suits waiting for us. My two white-robed escorts gestured me to exit, but the suits were standing in front of the elevators in such a way as to block the exit. I could play games too.

"Take me to your leader," I said practically, five inches from the face of the leading suit.

He stepped back, and composed himself. "Mr. Cruz, is it?" he said. "The Metro private detective. If you are here on behalf of Mr. Caret, then we will have to ask you to leave our religious sanctuary. The House has a restraining order against Mr. Caret and his company; and multiple slander and defamation suits are pending."

"Brother," I interrupted, "are you going to take me to your leader, or what?"

The suits looked at each other. Were they communicating telepathically? I grinned.

"Brother, it's cold down here. What's it going to be?"

From out of the shadows came one white-robed disciple after another. Before I knew it, I was surrounded by dozens of them.

"What's all this?"

No one spoke. They all just stared at me.

"Take me to Jed, or take me back up. I don't have time to play games with your cosmic cult."

The leading suit stepped up to me. "Cult? The House of Jed is not a cult, and we take any attacks in any form against the Master seriously."

"So, you're a violent group?"

"No, Mr. Cruz, we believe in complete non-violence at all times."

I ran through them like a power-bowling ball through a set of robot pins. It was a very long hallway, but it didn't take me long to get to the other end at the speed I was running. Inside the chamber looked like any cathedral—high ceiling, pews; at the front was a smaller version of the statue on the surface. It wasn't packed, but there were quite a few white-robed people sitting in the pews. Most looked to be in deep meditation, and others were reading some kind of electric notepad.

"Cruz, brother." I turned to see who was addressing me. The man was tall and lanky, dressed in a casual white suit, sandals, wearing dark shades. His long blond hair flowed down his waist. He had a mustache and beard, too. He walked to me and hugged me. I did not like strangers hugging me. He let me go. "I am the Master."

"We believe in the force of the universe."

We were sitting in some underground garden as the Master ate assorted chopped-up fruits from a bowl.

"We believe in good triumphing over darkness. We believe there are those who are born to fulfill a destiny. We believe in humankind's quest to trek across the stars to explore, seek out, learn, grow. We do not believe in forcing people to believe as we believe, we do not believe in holding people against their will, and finally, Mr. Cruz, we do not believe in draining the bank accounts of potential members. Did you know that Mr. Caret was once a member?"

"I didn't know that," I said.

"It's always the ex-members that are the most vocal detractors of our federation of good. Mr. Caret has hired you for a wild-goose chase."

"Where's the father?"

"He's at work, Mr. Cruz."

"Work?"

"Yes, Mr. Cruz. Work. We don't yet live in a universe free of the needs of money where you can sit idly by. We have day jobs like everyone else. Caret's father works as a cashier at our local Goodwill. He'll be here tomorrow morning. You can see him then."

"What day job do you have?"

"I work for Trash Services, and operate the trash compactors that turn the mountains of garbage this city produces every minute into recycling, fuel, and building material. Yes, Mr. Cruz, I believe my role as the spiritual leader of the House is the same. I remove all the trash and filth this world fills you with, and guide you to a life of simple basics, self-worth, and happiness."

"Aren't you a felon too?"

"Is that your background check, or Mr. Caret's? I was convicted of computer crimes and banned from using one ever again for the rest of my natural life. I am a human being too, and filled with as much trash and filth as the next person. Prison saved me. Being banned from computers saved me. My penance is to help others. There are a lot of bad people in the spirituality business, Mr. Cruz. I'm not one of them. I live in Free City, and all the money donated to the House sits in our bank account to help people and fight law suits. I'm not one of the bad guys here, Mr. Cruz. Your client is. He doesn't need you to get access to his father. So why did he hire you?"

CHAPTER 21

NeuroDancer

Much of private detective work was about instincts. What was true, and what was a pack of lies. The better you were at figuring out the difference, the more successful you could be, and, more importantly, the more likely you were to get to retirement without getting dead.

I believed Jed. I didn't necessarily trust his "I'm only here to help people" routine, but I felt he was being truthful at least in regards to Caret. When I recalled Caret's story, I knew it was Movie-Town fiction, but not all of it. Lies, truth, half-lies, half-truths.

Logo had invited me to an event. I hadn't planned to attend, but there I was. It wasn't a dance performance, but a fashion show. I almost felt that the only reason Logo had given me the tickets was as a false, reverse-psychology gesture; he never intended me to attend—but I did.

The show was in Downtown Metro, not too far from City Hall, and Metro Central at the ritzy Space Gate Hotel.

I really didn't know who NeuroDancer was, because I knew nothing about pop culture. Dot would know, but it was so last minute—I hopped in my Pony and went. I left the other ticket for PJ. My own gesture of reverse-psychology—PJ wouldn't go.

Before I even entered the hall I had a headache—no, a migraine. Loud music, flashing lights, people on top of each other. It was the typical set-up: catwalk runway, flanked by photographers and spectators. There was a bar at the back, but high-end waitresses kept the drinks coming to the tables.

"Cruz!" BetaMax patted my shoulder smiling as we passed each other in different directions.

I turned to see him disappear into the crowds. Who the hell was that guy?

I didn't sit. I mingled in the crowd, to see the world that Logo hung out in.

One model after another strutted down the runway, in all kinds of weird clothes masquerading as high fashion. The fashion show had a galactic theme, so the models had antennas from their heads, pointy ears, and a wide variety of sci-fi alien prosthetics. It was all silly to me, but then, I was not the audience, based on the "oohs," "ahhhs," and "oo la las" from the crowds.

Then it happened: every eye focused; the excess chatter stopped. The NeuroDancer appeared at the start of the runaway and stopped to be taken notice of. She was. Cameras flashed all at once, in an orgy of light and sound. People who were sitting rose to their feet. Everyone was clapping.

While everyone else was going weak in the knees, I did manage to notice the person who led her to the beginning of the runway, arm-in-arm. It was Mr. Logo.

CHAPTER 22

Rogue Two

Where did I go? The very place I said I didn't like to be at night. I went back to my Liquid Cool offices to grab a few files that I had forgotten in my impromptu stop at the Space Gate Hotel fashion show.

Logo was friends with NeuroDancer, too.

I exited my floor and started down the hallway. Well lit, but creepy. Not a living thing stirring, except for me. The elevator beeped and started back down to parking. Someone else was in the building. I stopped at my door with the key. I didn't enter. I walked back to the elevator and watched the numbers. They kept climbing to my floor. Was someone coming up to this floor? No.

I decided to go to the other end of the hallway and peek out from the corner. Just as I was about to run, I noticed the numbers of the other elevator were climbing. Two elevator cars were coming my way. I ran to the opposite hallway corner and waited.

Why was I being paranoid? This was a secure building. Decent security, though no human guards or doorman. I waited. A beep. A large man exited the elevator and walked down the hallway, stopping at the Liquid Cool office door. He knocked, and then rang the bell. A criminal wouldn't do that.

"Hey," I said, coming out from the corner. I startled him.

"You're Cruz, the private detective."

"Yeah, that's me, but it's after hours."

"I need to talk to you right away."

"I can get your information, but it will have to be tomorrow. How did you get into the building anyway? It's supposed to be locked to non-tenants."

I'm not sure which word set him off, but he drew, and started shooting at me. Every shot made a weird whistling sound. All I could do was throw myself down to the ground. My body was lethargic, my head woozy, and I didn't know why. I was being shot at *again,* and I was fumbling in my pocket for my weapon like an amateur.

When I did manage to aim my piece, I got off a shot, but the man was gone. I pulled myself to my feet, and looked around frantically. The man was gone. It was as if he'd vanished into thin air.

PART FOUR

The Five Rings of Babel Case

CHAPTER 23

China Doll

When you work with other people for a while, you get to know their moods. Today, PJ was acting weird. She normally had her French tunes playing, but it was all silence at her desk. She was working but it wasn't the same insufferable PJ.

For me, I had too much work to worry about employee mood swings. I had all these big cases stacking up. Mr. Caret's was still in process. Mr. Cruces' was still working. I wanted both cases done before the end of the week. I had a slew of minor cases too, and planned out my attack for the day. I was going to see Mr. Caret's father, and planned to wrap up at least two of the minor cases after that.

The whispering outside my office was getting irritating. I got up from my desk and walked out into the reception area. Dot! My wife and PJ were huddled at PJ's desk like scheming criminals.

"Dot," I said. "I didn't hear you come in."

She jumped up, smiled, ran to me, and gave me a kiss. "I wanted to surprise you."

"What are you two plotting?"

"Oh, nothing," she replied. "I do have to go, though."

"What? That's it?"

"Yeah."

"But, you just got here."

"Cruz, we do live in the same place, you know. You'll see me tonight. PJ and I needed to plan the surprise."

"Surprise? For who?"

"It's a surprise."

She smiled, and dashed out the door.

"What was that all about?"

PJ didn't answer me. She began typing whatever she was typing again with those speedy bionic fingers.

Before I could even sit back at my desk, I noticed PJ at my office doorway.

"I meant to ask before."

"What?"

"Did you hear about any shooting last night?" she asked.

"What shooting?"

"In the building," she answered.

"In the building, here? No. I didn't hear anything about that."

"Oh, never mind," PJ said. "People are always starting rumors."

CHAPTER 24

Caret Senior

I had now taken to pacing back and forth in front of the big-toe door of the House of Jed. Rain had never bothered me before, but I was in a foul mood. It was nearly two hours since I'd taken up my vigil, and still no Caret Senior.

Something told me to look in the crowd. I stopped and stared. Someone was staring at me. The man had a large, weird smile, and I didn't like it. It was Caret Senior all right.

"Hello, Mr. Caret," I said, now standing across from him.

"The son sent you, didn't he? The Master told me you'd be here. Did you have to wait long in the rain? I hope so. I did that on purpose. I wanted you to get good and wet. Which lie did the son tell you about me? He's quite the jokester. He thinks he's some kind of sky-walker, when, in fact, he's nothing but salacious scum."

Mr. Caret Senior was not going to stop. It was a never-ending tirade that went on and on. I noticed he was carrying a helmet. The geriatric was a hoverbiker.

"Why are you looking at my helmet? Are you going to take my helmet?"

"I'm not going to take your helmet. I only want to talk."

I almost slipped, getting out of the way of his swing. His helmet barely missed my head. Before I knew it, he was running into the crowds. He had put his helmet on, but his running was so slow, I'm not sure I'd call it running. I caught up to him, and tripped him. He crashed to the ground, and the sound of the helmet hitting pavement caused even me to wince. I turned him over; his breathing was labored.

"Is this helmet of yours made of space alloy?" I lifted his head a bit to take off the helmet.

When I did, he was staring at me with wide eyes, as if he didn't know who I was or where he was.

"Are you okay?"

The man was scared. "Help me."

"I will."

"Do you want Mr. Cruz to take you back to your son?"

I looked next to me. It was Master Jed, and all around us were his white-robed disciples.

"No. Please, no," Caret Sr. said. "All he wants are the plans to the weapon."

"Weapon?" I asked.

"Logo."

"What?" I asked. "What did you say?"

"Logo."

"What do you mean?"

"Kill Logo."

"Who wants to kill Logo?"

He began to drift out of consciousness.

"Mr. Caret, I need you to tell me," I said.

"Leave him alone," one of the female disciples snapped at me.

Master Jed stood up and directed his people to pick him up.

"Don't move him. Call an ambulance," I said.

"We have, Mr. Cruz, but maybe it would be more compassionate to get him out of the rain, and under some shelter. Or do you disagree?"

I did disagree, but they ignored me. It took six of the disciples to move Caret Senior to the doorway of their building. The hoverambulance arrived in moments. As we watched the medics take the man away, I shot Master Jed a look.

"Are you going to tell me what you know?"

"Mr. Cruz, you're the detective. I'm the crazy cult leader."

"Is that what this is about: I hurt your feelings? My Ma always used to say: As one adult to another, get over it. You don't want to help me? Let's see how fast I can get Caret Senior over to his son."

"I wouldn't do that."

"Why?"

"Mr. Cruz, have you done even the most basic background check on his son?"

"Actually, I have. I always do. Why?"

Master Jed suddenly got quiet. "Unfortunately, I may have said more than I should. Confessions are private."

"What? He told you something in confession, and you won't tell me. You're not a registered religious institution. You're a for-profit company."

"Then sue me."

"I don't want to sue you. I want you to tell me what you know." He was not budging. "You are so full of crap with your 'We are one with the force of the universe.' You know information to help one of your disciples, and you won't tell me, the police, or anyone. You know what, Master? Take your force and shove it."

CHAPTER 25

Caret

Mr. Caret was truly one of those center-of-attention, loud talkers. I recognized his voice right away, as he chatted it up with PJ in the reception area.

PJ appeared at the doorway.

"Your next appointment isn't here yet, so you can see this existing client."

"Send Mr. Caret in."

He strolled in, and the first thing I noticed was his Joker playing card neck tie. "Mr. Cruz!"

"Mr. Caret."

"How's my case going?"

"It's moving along. Have a seat, Mr. Caret."

"No, no. I won't be long." He closed my private office door. "Give me the quickie rundown."

"Met Master Jed. Met your father."

"You met Father? Did he try to kill you?"

"He tried."

"Now, that's Father!"

"Is there anything more to this case that I should know?"

"Mr. Cruz, I've given you all the relevant data for you to bring the case to resolution. Get my father out of the cult, and into my clutches. That's all you gotta do."

"Do you know a man named Logo?"

He didn't even need to respond. He was smiling like a loon, but I saw the flash of anger.

"What does he have to do with this?"

"Should we ask your father?"

Mr. Caret stepped to the chair in front of my desk, and sat down. "Mr. Cruz. Might there be something you'd like to discuss?"

"Is there anything more to this case that I should know about?"

"Not at all."

"How do you know Logo?"

"We know each other from way back. One of those 'knew each other a long, long, long time ago in a galaxy far, far, far away.' He's nothing."

"Okay."

"However, I did have another reason for stopping by. I think my life may be in danger."

"Why do you say that?"

"I had another attempt on my life yesterday."

"Another?"

"My thought exactly. Who would want to harm good ol' me?"

"How many other times?"

"A few."

"Police?"

"No need to bring them in."

"Who's behind it?"

"I'd like to hire you to find that out, but I have my suspicions."

"Who?"

"Logo, perhaps."

"A person you barely know anymore has tried to have you killed a few times?"

"He's jealous of me. Always has been."

"Jealous of what?"

"My success. My company. Everything I've done."

"Logo is after you. The House of Jed is after your father. As the Master would say, the force of the universe isn't smiling on you."

Caret laughed. "Yes, the fortune cookie wisdom of the House of Jed and his merry 'knights,' doing good in a galaxy near you."

"Mr. Caret, you hired me to help your father. That's what I'll do. If someone is trying to kill you, that's a matter for the police. Should I have my secretary dial the police for you."

"That won't be necessary. I'll be able to handle that."

"Mr. Caret, please. As someone who knows, and as someone who's had people try to kill them, call the police. Don't play games with this."

"Thanks for the advice, Mr. Cruz. I do appreciate it." He stood from his chair. "When do you think you'll be able to wrap up my case?"

"Now that I've met him—soon."

"Mr. Cruz, that's great! Great! Let me let you get to it."

Mr. Caret skipped to the door, opened it, and skipped out. I'm glad there wasn't a room full of clients waiting to see a grinning client skipping out of my office.

CHAPTER 26

Logo

I couldn't shake the feeling. Paranoia was actually a good disease in this business, but only in moderation. I feared I had crossed the acceptable line days ago. I felt I was being watched all the time, anytime I was outside the Concrete Mama, or the Liquid Cool office.

My hands tightly gripped my steering wheel as I alternated between my rearview and side view windows. I pulled the Pony into a pit-stop, and there I sat. Who was following me? The reality was, with all the hovercars in the sky, there was no way I could know if I were being followed. I had followed so many people myself as a detective. You could literally follow someone one length back in the sky lane above or below them, and they would never know. It applied to me too, even with my few anti-tailing gadgets. I couldn't shake the paranoia.

I powered up, and was about to fly back into the sky lane, when they pounced on me. Three souped-up hoverlimos descended on top of me, blocking my escape. My door was open; I already had gun in hand. I wasn't even going to try to have a conversation; I was going to start blasting the first face I saw.

"Mr. Cruz!" A hand popped out, and a young male, who looked to be in grade school, waved a white handkerchief around. "Please, Mr. Cruz. No danger."

"No danger? Do you always box people in with three vehicles like that? I could have shot you!"

"Yes, Mr. Cruz. We're sorry. We work for Mr. Logo. Please follow us, sir."

I was not happy, but I followed the three hoverlimos. We went to Elysian Heights to some Korean barbecue place—restaurant, bar, and dance club at night. It wasn't night, so when we entered, the dance floor was being used as a seniors' bingo tournament.

"Bingo!" an old woman yelled out.

The young man, and the other suits, led me to Mr. Logo.

"Why would you send guys to contact me like that? I could have shot them."

"Yes, Mr. Cruz. On reflection, not the wisest thing to do when dealing with a street detective accustomed to the more dangerous elements of Metropolis. Have a seat. Have you had lunch?"

"No, not yet." I sat, though still not in a good mood.

"There's plenty of food. Help yourself."

Korean barbecue was like an endless buffet, only the wait staff brought the food to you. Plates of Korean and Japanese cuisine were everywhere. With some food in me, I started to crawl out of my bad mood.

"Mr. Logo, what's wrong? Your case is going fine, and will be wrapped up soon."

"That's not why I wanted to see you so urgently, Mr. Cruz. My people said you received a visit from a Mr. Caret."

My paranoia wasn't a figment of my imagination.

"Why are you watching me, and why are you interested in him?"

"I am not watching you, Mr. Cruz. My people are watching him, though."

"Why?"

"He's trying to kill me, and has been for some time."

"Why?"

"We've been business rivals, for decades, but things have become more heated in recent years."

"Mr. Logo, call the police. That's what legitimate, normal people do."

"I need to know why he's resorting to these actions now. There's no reason for him to do this. We are not even in the same business industries anymore. I don't want to involve the police. I have legitimate interests, and police involvement will suggest otherwise to my client base and rivals."

"I don't like to take people's money for doing nothing. Even if I took the case, you know what I'd do."

"Call the police?"

"Exactly. There's no way around it, so you think about it. If that's acceptable, I can kick around and see what I can find out—but it will involve that call to Metro PD. That's unavoidable."

Logo sighed. "I'll ponder the matter further, and call you, Mr. Cruz."

"Yes, but don't send your men again like that. Call—and I'll call you when the other case is done."

"Agreed, Mr. Cruz."

CHAPTER 27

The Men From OC

I was driving back to the office when PJ called me on the video-phone.

"Are you coming back here now?" she asked.

"Yeah, why?"

"Metro Police called for you two minutes ago. They want you to go there."

"Chief Hub?"

"No, not him. Give the front desk your name when you get there."

I flew past Buzz Town and my offices on my way to Downtown. This time, I didn't look in my rear or side view mirrors. I accepted that I was being followed all the time, even if I wasn't.

I was thinking about Caret and Logo. Caret said Logo was trying to kill him. Logo said Caret was trying to kill him. Business rivals from the past? I liked paying clients. I could even excuse paying clients who were crooks. I didn't like paying clients who said they were legit, when it was obvious they were up to crooked things. Since I was going to be at Metro Police Central, I would try to see what the police knew. I always did background checks on all clients, since I didn't like surprises, but it was obvious my background checks on these two men were less than complete.

Most of the street police in Metropolis knew me, if not by sight, by reputation. Fortunately for me, it was a good reputation. You go after, and bring to justice a cop-killer, and you have police friends for life; just don't become a crazy criminal maniac yourself.

I was sitting in the lobby for only 10 minutes when an officer got me and led me to the elevators to another floor. He sat me in an interrogation room, which was not a good sign.

Two detectives entered in dark suits, and neither looked as if they were happy to see me.

"Mr. Cruz," one said. No handshakes. They sat down and threw their file folders on the table between us.

"That's me."

"Mr. Caret."

"Client."

"Doing what?"

"None of your business."

"Is that how you want to play this, Mr. Cruz?"

"How I want to play this? You called me down here. I came right away. Then, you plant me in a dirty interrogation room, and talk to me like I'm some kind of mutt. I'm not in a good mood today, and I'm in no mood for your nonsense. I'm out of here. I have work to do."

"Okay, okay, Mr. Cruz," one of them said, holding up a palm. "Let's start over."

"Who are you?"

"No names."

"What division, then?"

The detectives sat quiet for a moment. "Organized Crime."

I knew it. "Caret is a gangster."

"That's what we need you to tell us."

"What about Logo?"

From their expressions, I could see they were going to ask me about him too.

"Gangsters. There's nothing in their background checks about that."

"And there wouldn't be."

"Why would you scrub those facts from their file? People like me actually run background checks for a reason, like to find out if the person is a criminal."

"We're not in here to talk to you about background checks, but to find out what these two are up to, and to avoid a gang war."

"Gang war?" I shook my head. "How many gang wars am I going to be in the center of?"

They moved me to the clean, plush offices on the Organized Crime division floor. I got introduced to a few other detectives and one of the unit captains.

"Organized crime trying to sink its claws into the movie industry isn't anything new, and organized crime in politics? That's as old as politics. It's a revolving door. Yesterday's elected official is tomorrow's convicted hood, and vice versa," an unnamed detective informed me.

"We fear there may be a full-scale war in Metropolis between these two. They have diversified into legit businesses, but both are still in the illegal crime swamp. It's been a running battle between the two of them for years, sending hitmen and hit squads after their on-the-street bosses. Recently it's escalated to the men themselves," another detective added.

"Mr. Cruz, you can help us with this."

"Caret is trying to kill Logo, and Logo is trying to kill Caret?" I said.

"Yes. You seem doubtful."

"No, I believe you. I just don't believe Caret is trying to kill Logo, and vice versa."

"Why not?"

"How long have they been in crime?"

"Over 30 years each."

"Do you have gallery photos of all their known employees, associates, and rivals?"

The two detectives looked at each other, grinning.

"He's going to do that thing," one of them said.

"What thing?" I asked.

"We heard about you being able to look at photos, and identify criminals like that."

"I'm not Compstat Connie. Only she can do that, but maybe I'll see something. You know, a fresh set of eyes."

"Sure."

They sat me in another office at a computer screen and I scrolled through mugshots and photos. It seemed endless. Men, women, and even kid criminals through the ages—30 years' worth.

"There!" I said, but I believed in being thorough, so I continued my review for another hour, but I returned to the mugshot.

"Who's that?" I had called the detectives to the room.

"You know him?" the detective asked me.

"I've seen him a few times."

"He was a fellow gangster decades ago, but he went legit a long time ago. It's funny how easily some of these criminals can identify money-making ventures. He's making a killing in VR technology."

"The funny story about him," another detective said, "is that he was one of many gangster rivals that Caret and Logo 'encouraged' to leave the crime business and go legit. 'Encouragement'—thugs holding you down with a laser hacksaw swinging above your balls. That kind of encouragement."

"Beta Max," I said. "Why are you hanging around your former 'buddies'?"

CHAPTER 28

Punch Judy

As I headed back to Liquid Cool, I realized that I was married, and since getting back from our honeymoon and living in the same apartment, we had hardly seen each other.

That didn't make any sense. We both worked hard, but I felt Dot was doing something else separate from her work at Eye Candy. I was being paranoid again. I flew into the building parking lot off Circuit Circle, and I was almost positive I glimpsed Dot's dark silver hover-speedster bug zipping out of there.

"Was Dot here?" I asked PJ as soon as I walked into the office.

"Your wife?"

"PJ, that's the only Dot you know that I know."

"No, she wasn't here. Why do you ask?"

"Never mind. I thought I saw her hovercar driving out of the parking lot."

"Oh."

I walked to my private office. First, I realized it was the second day in a row that no one was waiting in the lobby. Secondly, and what made me stop, was a group of pictures of people on the wall. My eyes immediately locked on one man's face.

I walked to the picture, and tore it down from the wall. I turned around, and PJ was watching me, seated at her desk.

"What are all these pictures?"

"John Does from the police."

"Since when did you start hanging up John Does from the police on our wall?"

"They asked me to, but forget that. You know the man in your hand?"

I looked at the picture again. He was the man who'd shot at me that night, and disappeared into thin air. I looked up again at PJ.

"Bring the picture over," she said. "Let's see who he is."

I slowly walked to her desk, and handed her the picture.

PJ looked at some number on the back of the photo, and did her speed typing on her mobile computer. All the man's stats appeared. "Here we are," she said, and pointed to his name, then town.

I pointed to his occupation.

"An accountant!"

CHAPTER 29

Beta Max

I yelled out a string of orders to PJ. I wanted her to find out all about this accountant. Then I went into my office, and yelled, "I'll see what I can find out, too."

PJ was at my doorway. "No, you don't. You have client visits scheduled."

"Why aren't they scheduled for the office?"

"Because they don't want to come to the office. Paying clients. Messages are on your desk."

She disappeared, and I scanned the messages on the top of my desk looking at the names. *Beta Max!* I snatched the message.

I didn't even know there were office towers in Free City. The town where the five percent of the population that didn't have legacies lived, courtesy of the government. Free, government-style, always meant low quality and low class. That's exactly what I thought when I strolled into Beta Max's office, no name, only a number, with the Russian brunette secretary sitting outside his private office.

The secretary looked as if she could do a solid bench press set or a dozen.

"Mr. Cruz, how the hell are you?" He was so glad to see me, jumping up from behind his desk to shake my hands. "Glad we could finally meet."

"We've bumped into each other a few times."

"Yes, we have. Have a seat."

As I sat, he went behind his desk, and pulled his chair out from behind, to place right across from my chair.

"You don't remember me, do you?" he asked.

"We've bumped into each other before?"

"It was the Tronic Light-Cycle Race Extravaganza."

I nodded. "I remember now. I think that was the only hovercycle race show I went to as a new youth entrepreneur. It was fun, but I liked the clientele at hovercar shows better."

"You were right to think that. Classic hovercar collectors spend a hell of a lot more money than hoverbike collectors. It's a simple matter of business."

"Were you one of the racers?"

"I was. Rode in more than my fair share of races. Won a lot of trophies, cash prizes, but far more trips to the local hospital, with all the crashes. Not a sport for anyone but youth. I could have continued, but by now, I would've been all cyborg. Brutal sport. Fun, but brutal."

"What's your business now?"

"That's why I wanted you to come down, or at least one of the reasons. VR, Mr. Cruz!"

I was not impressed. "I'm not a big virtual reality guy."

"VR has lots of practical uses."

"I agree. I spend a lot of time in the shooting games."

"Smart. Hone those quick draw, shooting skills. Smart. All the VR shooting games on the market are as good as any law enforcement simulation. I never bothered with that part of the market. Established players, and the profit margin was too low."

"Games then?"

"Lots of games, Mr. Cruz. Five Rings of Babel is what put me on the map. That was our flagship VR game from 20 years ago. But we're always coming out with new ones. We have the hottest games out there."

"Just the games. What about the worlds?"

"We consider the VR world market a different animal. People live in VR worlds. We cater to the hardcore gamers only."

"What did you want to talk about?"

"I called you down here to hire you, Mr. Cruz."

"What's the problem?"

"Unfortunately, in my youth, I wasn't only a wild hoverbiker and peri-terrestrial sky jumper. I was a bit too wild on the criminal side too. However, I left all that behind—too busy being rich."

"Here in Free City?"

He laughed. "Yes, Mr. Cruz. Here in Free City. Do you know Free City has the highest percentage of VR gamers than any other place in Metropolis?"

That didn't surprise me in the least.

"I set up shop where my customers live. It adds to the appeal—and the profits."

He got all serious on me, and wrung his hands.

"What's wrong?" I asked.

"I think the criminal element is after me, or more precisely, my business. There are two crime bosses, that's what I'm told, trying to muscle into the Free City rackets. Now, I'm not naive. I know there's a lot of crime here in Free City. They've got their gangs, but there's lots of good people here. Kids and families. People trying to get by. These two crime bosses have been turning up the violence. They're fighting each other for control. I find myself in the middle, and I don't know what to do. These are dangerous men. If the Free City gangs are terrified of them, I'd be a fool not to be terrified of them too."

"What would you like me to do?"

"I'm nobody—rich guy, yes—but I'm in Free City, with no connections at all. Mr. Cruz, you have plenty of connections. You know the cops. If I call them to complain about these crime bosses, they'll ignore me. More importantly, I could be putting my life, and my employees' lives in jeopardy. But if you contact the police and tell them what's going on, they'll listen."

"Mr. Max, you're hiring me to call 9-1-1 on your behalf."

"You got it!"

CHAPTER 30

Bite-Size

I could not believe what I'd done. I took the man's money to do nothing. Of course, the two crime bosses he was fingering were Caret and Logo. The police already knew about them. Yes, I pocketed money for nothing. PJ would be proud, but I can't say that I was. The real reason I did it was I didn't like Beta Max at all. He told me he was at those establishments that we bumped into each other at to check out these crime bosses, try to figure a way out of his predicament without having to resort to the police. Did I believe him? No.

PJ called me on the Pony's dashboard. Her face watched me from the display.

"I got it!" she exclaimed.

"Who did the accountant work for?"

I saw her eyes reading from her electric steno-pad. "He worked for at least two movie studios."

This was officially not a joke anymore. Two different accountants, who worked for movie studios, had tried to whack me.

"When was a Missing Person's report filed, then?"

I could see PJ hesitating. "There hasn't been any yet."

"Wait. How did you get his picture then?"

"I saw him on our video surveillance from last night. He broke into the building. I called the police on him, and other people in the building did, too. Cruz, I have contacts at the police, too."

"How do you have police friends?"

"I do, because of you. Anyway, they went to arrest him, and that's when they told me he'd disappeared."

"Well, you're not missing until at least 72 hours. We're jumping the gun by two days."

"There's more."

"What?"

"They did find a John Doe body that they think is him."

"Body?"

"They found it at one of the landfills. It was pure luck that they found it."

"You'll have to tell me more about all of that later. Is the body his, or not?"

"The body has no face and no fingertips, Cruz."

"No face?"

"Someone burned it off with acid, and the fingers were cut off."

What PJ was describing was depraved violence. Most criminals, even the bad ones, didn't mutilate corpses like that.

"PJ, is it the police saying the body may be his or you saying that?"

"Well—me saying so."

"Just the facts, PJ. I need some expert help on this one."

Bite-Size was a kid. Roly-poly body, spectacles, and he smoked. He also ran the Netsite Movie-Town Madness. He knew more about movies than anybody. It was my associate, Phishy, who had introduced us. The kid apparently loved detective movies, and felt I was a shoo-in to have the movie industry make a movie or series about me. That's what he told me when he asked for my autograph. He said my signature was worthless now, but if and when a movie or series happened, he'd have a piece of gold.

"No smoking!" PJ scolded him. "Read magazines if you're bored."

Like all kids, he frowned at her from the reception lobby, sitting and restless. His legs didn't even touch the floor.

"Where is he?" I walked in to hear him ask.

"Cruz!" He jumped up.

I saw he was wearing a Liquid Cool T-shirt, and I frowned.

"I'm going to ask you a question, but I'm going to make it a hypothetical."

"Okay, I can play."

Bite-size had moved the chair closer in front of my desk before he sat. I was leaned back in mine.

"Once upon a time, there was this—reporter snooping around to get a story. He met with a few studio heads, then—bam! A movie studio accountant tried to shoot him, and got shot dead by police for his trouble. The reporter thought it was a freak accident, mistaken identity. Then bam! Another accountant tried to kill him."

Bite-size wasn't smiling at all. "Mr. Cruz, are you being serious right now?"

"It's a hypothetical."

"I'm a kid, not a retard. Are you being serious now?"

"I called you here to my office, didn't I?"

"Movie studio accountants are trying to kill you?"

"I am not saying that. I'm asking, in this hypothetical story I gave you: Why would two accountants try to kill the reporter?"

"Because the accountants thought the reporter stumbled upon some movie studio scam worth galactic-size bags of cash."

"What studio scam?"

"I don't know. I'm not a detective."

I took a piece of paper from a side drawer and wrote two names on it.

"This is confidential," I said, and could see the anticipation in his face. "I know nothing about movies. You know everything. I don't have time to learn everything about the movies, when I have movie studio accountants trying to whack me. I'm busy with other cases. Find out every movie these guys worked on and see if you see something. You say movie studio scam. What? What could it possibly be?"

"Did the attempts happen before or after you visited a particular studio?"

"I'm impressed, kid. That's what's called a brilliant question. After."

"Which one?"

"Body Shot Studios."

"I'm on it."

"Don't tell anyone what you're doing, and if you figure it out, find me immediately."

CHAPTER 31

Beta Max

"Mr. Cruz, I desperately need your help. It's gone from bad to worse. A bunch of thugs broke into my main attorney's house. They beat him up, and his wife, to send me a message. Those two crime bosses want me to turn over all rights to the Five Rings of Babel to them. That VR game accounts for half my company's profits, but I can't fight crime bosses. They've threatened my life; now they've beaten my attorney and his wife. I'm scared, Mr. Cruz. I need help. Police help. Your help. I need help."

Beta Max's video-call message was waiting for me when I came out of my meeting with Bite-Size. PJ said Beta Max didn't want to hold, or call back. He'd just wanted to leave that message.

PART FIVE

The Gangsters of SAG

CHAPTER 32

Union Hovertruckers

"When are you getting back to the office?" PJ was on my mobile.

"Why? You know where I am," I replied.

"Cruz, you need to get back *tout suite*. It's a surprise that is going to put the biggest smile on your face."

"I need those kinds of surprises. Big check, huh?"

"Big check, and many more to come, but you need to get back to the office."

"I'll be back as soon as I'm finished with my new client here."

"New client? Wives don't count as clients. They don't have to pay."

Yep, the client was the wife. I don't know where it came from, but she wanted me to accompany her to a meeting. She swore it wasn't bodyguard work, but I had to go with her.

Unions.

There were plenty of government gangsters. I had the displeasure of meeting a whole bunch of them, and I even had several as clients. Corporations had their own gangsters, but they were more of the military mercenary type. If either were a separate planet, unions would be the moon that spiral orbited both.

Why was Dot meeting the fattest, slimiest, greasiest lot of them at their headquarters?

Dot worked at Eye Candy, the exclusive image salon in trendy, upper-scale Paisley Parish. Clients came from all over Metropolis to get made up to look a movie star. They had to keep an appointment calendar a year out, and slots were always booked fast. That's how popular the establishment was.

But the wife was also an organizer. Up-Top and "down-below" were different animals. Up in space, people liked robots and automation. Here on Earth, you'd better be careful. "Them robots, ain't taking our jobs." That probably was the real reason there were so many cyborgs. People were not going to let robots take away human jobs. Unions were going to see to it, and Dot with her colleagues were forming their own union that was going to make sure they didn't take away any fashionista jobs. Eye Candy was the driving force. Robots could help humans, but not replace them when it came to jobs.

I can't say I had much sympathy for the movement. Pay 10 times the price to have some glittered-up hairdresser cut my hair, and take two hours to do it? Or use a pair of clippers that I could buy off some sidewalk johnny for nothing, and cut my own hair in five minutes? Obviously, my answer was choice number two, but I would never tell Dot that, lest I find myself sleeping out in the gutter, in the rain.

Even so, all people needed their cause. Mine was private eye-ing. This was hers.

Dot was here for advice. She knew she'd be going up against some very powerful interests in Silver City, and even Silicon Dunes. She needed advice. These union thugs could provide that.

"What's he here for?" one of the union thugs asked.

We were sitting in a dark, dank office. The union boss was in the middle; two sets of guys sat on either side. They represented the Hovertruckers Union. Why Dot chose to meet with them, I had no idea. I actually did know people in the Trash Union who, compared to these bozos, were a better class of union thug.

"He's along for the ride," Dot answered. "You felt we should join a union rather than start a new one?"

"Yeah," the boss said. "We've got all these small unions all over the place. Small means less power. Look at the megacorps. They've got the Council of Corporations."

"Isn't that more to take advantage of each other?"

"No, it's to be able to stand up to the government."

"Hey, mute. What do you think?" The same thug was directing his question to me. Thugs never liked me. Maybe because I didn't like them.

"I think you're a lug," I said.

I could see Dot smile from the corner of my eye.

"Lug? What's a lug?" the boss said to me—not asking a question, but to taunt me.

"My husband is messing with you," Dot said.

"Husband?" the boss said. He leaned back, grabbed something from his shirt pocket, and put on a pair of super-thick glasses. "I knew I recognized that hat. You're that private detective. What's his name?"

He looked at his men and they all looked at each other thinking.

One snapped his fingers. "Cruz!"

"Cruz."

"Yeah, Cruz!"

"Cruz."

These were the mental giants my wife was consulting with.

"You're married to the world-famous Cruz," the union boss said.

"No," I said. "I'm married to the world-famous China Doll."

"He does talk!" that union thug yelled and started chuckling.

"Yes, you are," the boss said. "Here's the thing, Doll. Look at all the industries in your vertical. They've got unions. Join 'em. At the very least, have your leadership do so. Then look at all the industries similar to you, your horizontal, where there might be some synergy. That's where you form your union. Think big. You're building an army, not a social club. Think about it like that. Forget about people liking you. You want them to fear you, Doll. No offense, but hairdressers, tailors, and stylists don't scare people."

"But, have they seen my boots?" Dot asked.

The union slobs looked down at my wife's feet. The boots she was wearing had some seriously menacing pointy heels.

"I've killed people with these boots! You also know my boss, Prima; have you seen that face when she gets mad? Do you know what she can do with a pair of scissors in those hands, when she's mad?"

The men started laughing.

"Yeah, you don't want Prima mad at you," the boss said.

"Stomp 'em," another one of them yelled, pretending to stomp an imaginary person with his fat feet. "Take that, you bum."

"Well, Doll, let's show you around. When you make your union, you have to make sure your headquarters is a fortress. Both the megacorps and the government will try to fill the place with surveillance bugs spying on you. You see a cockroach, and it may not actually be a cockroach. One of their surveillance devices may be crawling away on its own. They have robots to spy on us, and robots to steal our jobs."

"We'll leave a bloody robot's head next to them in their bed when they wake up. That's the robots we like," another said.

Charming.

They led us on the tour of the "facility," or what I called a dump. I don't know why they bothered, since the rest of the place was as dim and dank as their boss's main office.

CHAPTER 33

Tuck Rogers and Perfect Tony

When I got back to the Liquid Cool offices, I thought there had been another shooting or act of crime. People were congregated in the hallway. Some of them recognized me as I brushed past people. Inside, there were more people, and I saw PJ entertaining Tuck Rogers and Perfect Tony. I didn't know much about pop culture. I knew sub-cultures, like hovercars, crime (i.e., identifying criminal maniacs), private investigation. I didn't know much about the movie world, but I immediately recognized the major movie stars standing in my office.

"There he is!" PJ almost jumped. "Cruz, come over here." She grabbed me with a bionic arm.

"Mr. Cruz, it's a pleasure." The older actor, Tuck Rogers, didn't shake my hand; he gave me a fist bump.

"Cruz," Perfect Tony said, with a wave of the hand.

All around us were all these young women.

"Our entourage," Tuck said to me.

"Good for you. You don't ever have to go to clubs, or log onto the Net."

I looked at PJ.

"They're not clients. Well, they won't be normal clients," she said.

"Didn't the studio casting office arrange this for you, Mr. Cruz?" Tuck asked.

"Hmm. Let me consult with my office manager," I said, and pulled PJ into my private office, and closed the door. Now she had me referring to her as "office manager," rather than secretary.

"Don't get mad," PJ said. "Movie-Town movie stars. How could I say 'No?' It must be referrals from your movie studio cases."

"PJ, what are they hiring me to do?"

"Nothing."

"Hiring me to do nothing?"

"They're doing a new movie. They want to follow you around on your cases."

"What?"

"Yes. What is that called, when you ride with the cops?"

"Ride-along."

"Yes. They'll be your ride-alongs."

"I can't have famous movie stars running around with me on the street while I'm doing my private investigating work."

"Cruz, are you crazy? Look at this!"

She went to my desk and logged on. How she also logged into the Liquid Cool business account, I had no idea. I had to admit the deposit was of an amount I was not accustomed to.

"This is only the first one!"

"The movie will be out next summer," Tuck said. He was in the passenger seat of the Pony, and Perfect Tony was in the back, sitting in the middle. "The studios feel we can ride a wave of new public interest in the detective genre, namely because of you."

"Me?"

"Mr. Cruz, the studios have been sitting on these stories for years. They're green-lighting them now because of your cases in the public. No reason you can't ride the wave too. The hat—priceless."

"The studios love the fedora. My character will be wearing one, too," Perfect Tony added.

"Your character? You're playing the detective?"

"I told them I didn't want to play what the studios thought a real detective was like. I wanted to become a real detective. They gave me a list of 20 detectives to shadow. I saw your name, and that was it for me. You're the real detective I want to be. That's what I'm bringing to the movie."

I couldn't believe I was going to have a major movie actor using me as his model for a character.

"Who will you be playing in the movie, Mr. Rogers?" I asked.

"Call me Tuck. Everyone does. I'm going to be the police chief of the supercity."

I burst out laughing. "You're going to be Hub? You're too good-looking to be him."

All Tuck said was, "It's a movie. Even the ugliest people are played by good-looking actors."

I had to be very careful. Even without my recent bout of paranoia, private investigation work was dangerous. What would happen if a major movie star, in my care, was shot by some criminal aiming for me? I could kiss Liquid Cool goodbye.

Tuck was a straight professional, who spent most of the time asking me questions about the private eye business. Perfect Tony, on the other hand, was this big Method actor and watched every nuance about me: how I talked, walked, mannerisms, everything. If I had smoked, he would have copied how I held the cigarette, and how I took a puff. I expected the next time I saw him, he'd be in a tan fedora and slicker just like me.

Since I had a slew of small cases to knock out, I felt comfortable bringing them along. No trade secrets would be revealed, and they would be nowhere near my more confidential cases. For all their talk about the craft, my two Movie-Town stars would only be with me for a couple of hours. That was their idea of a day of hard work. I knew they really wanted to get back to their groupie entourage.

Our first stop was near Nil Point. I realized so many of my cases were someone wanting me to find someone else, which often meant I was dealing with shady clients. There was often a good reason a person didn't want to be found. But this was a case where all involved were angels. Mother had given up a child for adoption at 15. Twenty years later, she wanted me to track the child, and simply ask if she cared to see her birth-mother. The "child"— a cute 20 year old —first told me "Hell, no!" Two days later, she called back, and said, "Heavens, yes!"

In two hours, I expected to make three stops and see three different clients. It was an hour later, and we were still in Mech City with the "child." Tuck followed my instructions, and remained in the Pony, but Perfect Tony followed me anyway. The crazy actor was walking the way I walked. She answered the door, saw me, saw Perfect Tony, stared at Perfect Tony, and fainted.

"We have to get on the road!" I yelled.

The "child" already had four children of her own—all girls. First, it was the autographs, then how they had seen every one of his movies—multiple times, how they were his greatest fans, and couldn't wait to see his next movie. I wanted to vomit.

"We're going!" I yelled. "The Pony express is leaving now!"

Perfect Tony had to go there. He gave each of her children hugs, enabling the psychosis. I should have smacked him. We finally got the "child" in the Pony, after she'd almost fainted again at seeing Tuck. She was practically sitting in Perfect Tony's lap. Tuck was asking her all kinds of questions, each one having to do with me—how I'd contacted her, questions I'd asked. Were they going to use my exact conversation in the movie script? I was thinking like PJ now. I'd better get paid!

It was an hour and 15 minutes later when we finally made it to the birth-mother's place in Riggings Square! Tuck didn't stay in the Pony this time. Here I was knocking the door with the distinguished Tuck Rogers on one side, and Perfect Tony holding hands with the "child."

My birth-mother client opened the door. She saw me, saw Tuck Rogers, stared at Tuck Rogers.

"Don't do it!" I yelled.

She fainted.

I had to go through it all over again, this time, with the mother.

CHAPTER 34

The Politician

Needless to say, I was only able to do one stop in two hours. No wonder it took so long to make a movie. Movie stars made everything move slower. Fortunately, it was only two hours, and their next availability to ride-along with me wasn't going to be for another week or so. Good; I could get some work done.

It left the rest of the day for me to work on my major cases. I dropped my two movie stars at some high-end eatery in Silicone Dunes, and was free of them. I enjoyed their company, but the way I was made, I could take them for only short periods of time.

As for my clients? What a way to be reunited—with your favorite movie celebrities at your door. They'd be chatting about Tuck and Perfect Tony all day and night for days, weeks, and months to come. They wouldn't remember me, or the fact they'd been apart for 30 years.

I was back at the Cruces' palatial residence. As the butler led me down the hallway to his office, I sensed something—I turned and noticed there were two men in suits, sitting in separate chairs, watching me pass by. One was older, and both were wearing very expensive calf-high boots. I didn't know footwear the way my wife did, but I did know those, because I'd tried to buy a pair once, and had laughed when I saw the price. The men sat in what was like a cul-de-sac in the wall, but behind a large statue. I only saw them, because I happened to look back.

"Mr. Cruz," the butler said to me.

I turned around and followed him.

Cruces came into the room. "Mr. Cruz," he said. I was waiting with the same three aides that I'd seen on my last visit. We did the standard greetings, and he sat across from us.

I handed him a folder. He used his crossed legs as a kind of table, and reviewed the contents.

"Any problems, Mr. Cruz?"

"None at all."

"You're confident that I'll be unable to find them?"

"I am."

"What about you?"

"At this point, there's more than 10 degrees of separation between me and them. I can't find them, so you can't, and neither will any of your rivals."

He nodded and closed the folder.

"The only wild card is that none of them do anything stupid," I added.

"Such as calling me on the phone."

"That would qualify as stupid."

He smiled. "None of them are stupid."

"Then it's done."

"Good, Mr. Cruz." He gestured at one of his aides with his index fingers. "Give Mr. Cruz his payment."

"How's your campaign?"

"Excellent. Thanks for asking."

"I couldn't help noticing two gentlemen waiting in your hallway."

His eyes looked down, and he frowned a bit.

"I told them to wait, sir," one of the aides spoke up.

Cruces nodded.

"What political firm are you using?" I asked.

"Are you planning on running for something, Mr. Cruz?"

"That would be a—never. No, but a colleague is considering it. Oh, don't bother yourself. I can get their info from your aides."

"Oh, no bother, Mr. Cruz. The firm is called—Prime—um—Prime—something. No, it's called Prime Politics. Something like that. But they're extremely expensive."

"I may not be of wealth, but my colleague is. But if it's one of the majors, he'll know."

"Don't tell me your friend Run-Time is considering politics?"

We were standing now, and one of the aides handed me an envelope with cash.

"You know my friend, Run-Time? No, not him. He'll never run for anything either. No, someone else. Anyway, it's not important. I'm glad I could add another satisfied client to the Liquid Cool list."

"You have, Mr. Cruz. Fast, efficient, and discreet. I'll be sure to send business referrals your way."

"Thanks, Mr. Cruces. I do appreciate that."

The butler led me out of the room. The two men in the cul-de-sac area were not there on my way out. I did hear yelling from behind us, as if someone were throwing a tantrum. The butler quickened his pace. He couldn't get me out of the residence fast enough.

CHAPTER 35

China Doll

What politician running for Federal office, any office, didn't know the name of the firm helping them get elected? I knew nothing about politics, but I knew about that. Why did he lie to me? You solve the client's case quickly, efficiently, and they still lie to you.

I had no time to figure out why. It was one of those many unanswered questions to add to the "when I'm bored out of my mind and have nothing to do" list. The list I kept, but rarely had a chance to tackle. It wasn't important. I had real cases to occupy my attention.

Now, I was off to the wife's work, Eye Candy.

Eye Candy Image Salon was always packed with customers, from the time it opened, until its late-night closing. Women came from every corner of Metropolis for their "fashion police" of makeup artists, hairdressers, manicurists, pedicurists, skincare techs, tattoo artists, wardrobe stylists, and even dressers to assemble their wardrobe, if needed. The establishment was owned by Prima Donna, the Matron Queen of Metropolis fashion, who still had the magic touch, after so many decades and personally tended to their oldest and highest-tipping clients.

My wife, China Doll, was Prima's number one and was boss in her absence. Like every other fashionista employee, she wasn't some by-the-hour laborer. This was a coveted and highly competitive career; everyone who worked in the parlor had advanced degrees in beauty and skincare, fashion and style arts, health, and nutrition.

The interior of Eye Candy was designed like a beehive; every section was visible, due to its transparent walls, to every other section, except for the break room, full body baths, and the bathrooms. Eye Candy was nothing but carefully coordinated chaos. Women sat on chairs getting their hair and makeup done in one section, their nails and toenails in another, facials in another, tattoos in another (always temporary, to change according to current fashion trends), skincare consultations in another, and style analysis wardrobing in yet another section.

"Were you saving all these questions?" Dot asked me.

"Yeah," I answered. "Now, tell me about this NeuroDancer."

"Cruz, you really don't know who she is?"

"No."

"She's only the most famous dance performer on the planet."

"Movie star?"

"She's more famous than movie stars, and makes a lot more money than them."

"She just dances? That's it?"

Dot began giggling. "Dancing, that's it? No, Cruz, not dancing. Dance performance. Big shows all over the world, and Up-Top. They're big events."

"She's famous for doing what you and I do on dance night at the Booty Shaker."

"That's dancing. What she does is dance performance. Big difference. No one is going to pay us millions for dancin' to old songs."

"She's famous for dance performance. Got it. I think I got it. I got it, but I don't understand it. I don't get pop culture."

"You get pop culture fine. I can't believe you don't know her."

"Other than seeing her a few times, that's it. Never knew the history."

"What did you think of her dancing?"

I frowned. "I haven't seen one of her shows yet. Who is she dating?"

She gave me a look. "Why?"

I gave her a look back. "'Cause I want to know."

"She dates lots of guys, is what I hear."

"Yeah—and from what I see, the rumors are true."

"Before you ask, I wanted you to accompany me because I had heard the Hovertruckers Union can be a bit on the shady side. With a famous detective at my side, business would remain business-like."

"Me though. Why didn't you bring your posse?"

"My posse?"

"They're more formidable than me. Pinkie, Goat Girl, Cyan."

"They'll be flattered you think they're formidable, but they're not famous. You are. Besides, it's good to be able to keep an eye on you."

CHAPTER 36

Master Jed

I left the wife there after saying goodbye to all the Eye Candy people, which always took about an hour. Fashionistas loved to talk, and suck you into their stories.

As I drove back to my office in the Pony, the men from Organized Crime called me. When I told them I had nothing new to tell them, they seemed not to believe me.

"I gave you everything I've got," I said. "What else were you expecting? Is there something you'd like to share with me?"

"No, Cruz. Just remember you're dealing with gangsters, and not businessmen," one of them said.

"Don't worry about that. I never forget a gangster is a gangster, no matter how harmless they seem, and how much they smile at me."

The first of his robed "knights" came up to my office, and PJ immediately buzzed me. By the time I had stepped out of my private office, there were about half a dozen of them in the reception area. PJ wasn't messing around, and grabbed her laser shotgun from under her desk.

"We are a universal movement of peace," said one disciple.

"I am a universal cyborg of destruction, if you do anything I don't like," PJ snapped back at her.

I stood in the hallway, and the robed "knights" lined the walls of the hallway as their man walked out of the elevator towards me. Master Jed.

I let him, and only him, into my office. I stood while he came in and sat down in front of my desk. I hung back, and slowly walked to my desk. He didn't wait.

"I want to hire you, Mr. Cruz."

"Hire me? I already have a client. A client who's accusing your organization of brainwashing his father."

"Mr. Cruz, if you're truly as intelligent as everyone says you are, then you no more trust Caret than you trust—me. Mr. Caret has a—dark side."

I sat back down at my desk. "Like you."

"Like you."

"What do you want, Jed?"

"We're not some 'evil empire,' as others try to portray us."

"Yes, you're just the rebellion of all things good and of the light."

Jed enjoyed me mocking him.

"Davey, Caret's father, was in hospital care. He still is. But apparently, someone broke into the facility. They stole all his belongings."

"Okay. Sounds like a job for the police."

"Mr. Cruz, in a supercity of murder, rape and mayhem, the police aren't going spend a second on simple theft. Good news for detectives like you. We will pay you to locate those belongings."

"Someone broke in and stole his wallet and stuff, and you want me to find that? I'll save you some money and time. No one can find that. It's long gone. All of it. That kind of stuff disappears in seconds on the street."

"The House of Jed is not interested in a wallet and trifles. We want you to recover the helmet."

"Are you a hoverbiker, Master?"

Jed smiled. "In the metaphysical universe, hoverbiking is like riding the very waves of its force. I'm a collector, actually. How much would you like us to pay you?"

CHAPTER 37

Caret

I was so glad to get Jed and his white-robed "knights" out of my office, and out of the hallway of my building. PJ and I watched them go on the surveillance monitors at her desk.

"We're letting a potential paying client go," I said to her, watching the screens.

"No, I agree with you now," she said. "We have to be more discriminating with our paying clients. If they come to the office with 50 people with them, then they're an absolute 'No!'"

"Hello, Mr. Caret," I said.

His smirking face stared at me from the video-phone screen.

"You're playing jokes on me, Mr. Cruz."

"I did what you asked me to do, even after he tried knocking my head off with his helmet."

"Did you, Mr. Cruz?"

"I did. He's at Metro General, resting, under mental supervision."

"The hospital that these religious nuts in robes sent him to."

"Mr. Caret, the House of Jed doesn't own Metro General Hospital, or any of its staff. If you know where he is, why haven't you gone to collect him? I set up everything for you. The House of Jed sent their lawyers over there to try to get him to sign over power of attorney to them, but I got there first and let the hospital staff know what they were up to. You're the decider, Mr. Caret. Go get him, and put him in Metro Asylum like you said you would."

"I'm so glad you only have my best interests in mind. I did send my people over to visit him, and I was most distressed to learn that an institution as prestigious as Metropolis General Hospital is plagued like the common corner pharmacy with robberies. They stole my dear old father's things."

"What things? His clothes? Wallet?"

"No. I was interested in his helmet. It has a lot of sentimental value for me."

"Did you want your father, or his hoverbike helmet? You need to make up your mind. I told your friend, Master Jed, when I declined his case to find the helmet, I'm not going to chase through a city of 50 million people looking for a damn helmet. You have the money. Buy a new helmet. He can wear it when you put him in the asylum."

Caret watched me quietly for a while.

"Is there anything else, Mr. Caret?"

"I guess I'd better go collect my dear old father. Consider me another satisfied customer. However, his helmet was a birthday present from yours truly. It can't be replaced. I'll let it all hang out on the table. Should it come into your possession, there will be a fat, very fat, finder's fee in it for you."

"Why didn't you just say that at the start? I'm a private detective, and a businessman too. Of course, if I hear anything, you'll get the first call."

"That's what I wanted to hear, Mr. Cruz."

"Have fun making your movies."

"Mr. Cruz, if you were to lock me in a room all by myself, in a straight-jacket, in the dark, I'd still be able to make my own fun. Bye!"

CHAPTER 38

Logo

I didn't like it at all. I had tried to call Run-Time a couple of times, but he was unreachable. His staff said he was at a private business retreat, and wasn't taking any outside calls. In all the many years I had known my best friend, he was never unreachable. He had had plenty of secret business meetings, but family and friends could always contact him. He was the kind of boss that made time for family and friends.

Phishy was another one I tried to reach. He was "out of town." Phishy was never out of town. Even if he went on some quick vacation you could get him on his mobile, or his friends would get a hold of him for you. He was a street hustler. Street hustlers were always hustling. There were no vacations, and there was no being unreachable. I was suspicious.

"PJ, I want you to find out where they are," I directed her, as I began to leave the office.

"You left messages for them."

"Yes."

"Then they'll call you."

"PJ, find them. I need to talk to them."

"Okay, okay. I'll find them. Where are you going?"

"When did you start wanting to know where I'm going? Out. Errands. There's no one on the schedule. Where are all our clients? The reception area has been pretty empty lately."

"You've had all these paying clients, real clients, and you complain about a brief respite in the reception area? We just had 50 people in here. They'd better not be naked under those white robes."

"Okay. I'll be back later, but don't wait for me. Lock up if I don't get back."

"I always do."

I recognized the three souped-up hoverlimos hovering near the entrance of the parking lot. As I drove the Pony out, the window of one slid down, and the same young kid popped out to wave to me. It was Logo's son again.

I pulled up the Pony as I rolled down my own windows. I had my gun on my lap.

The rear window of one of the hoverlimos rolled down its window. "Mr. Cruz," Logo said, sitting in the back.

"Mr. Logo."

"I was told you'd successfully concluded the case of our politician."

"I did."

"Very good."

"I aim to please. Anything else?"

"Have you given any further consideration to the matter of Mr. Caret?"

"Mr. Logo, I told you to call the police."

"What is this matter about a...helmet? Rumors are that Mr. Caret, and others, are anxious to obtain it."

"I don't know anything about it."

"I heard it was stolen from Metro General. Shocking how lax our government institutions are. People can't even be cared for at a hospital without having their personal effects stolen by the common criminal."

"Not all of us can afford private luxury hospitals. What can I do for you, Mr. Logo?"

"Caret wants that helmet. Then I want that helmet. I know he would have offered a finder's fee. I'll triple it. Whatever he offered."

"I'll consider it. Anything else?"

"Oh, yes." He leaned forward, smiling. "I also hear you're becoming friends with movie stars. Get me Tuck Rogers' and Perfect Tony's autographs, and I'll buy them from you."

I smiled. "Okay, Mr. Logo. I'll work on that one too."

I rolled up my window and flew off in the Pony.

CHAPTER 39

Rogue Three

I needed Phishy, but couldn't get a hold of him. I needed to consult with Run-Time and couldn't get in touch with him, either. I wanted to wrap up these cases. I drove, and nothing more. No music, just quiet, the sky, and my thoughts. At the moment, I had so many loose threads of open and recently closed cases, that I needed a break.

I was tempted to call Bite-Size, but if he had anything, he'd find me. I was bored. Bored people often do dumb things, and I didn't want to do anything dumb, or get shot.

My eyes glanced at my side and rearview displays. Sure, I could have been followed. The rain was coming down hard; it was dark, but the traffic was a bit lighter than normal. I shifted into different sky lanes periodically, but never saw anyone around me change positions.

I rose into the fast lane, and I floored it. Classic muscle hovercars could accelerate faster than most jets. That's how fast I was flying, out of one town after the next, on the freeway. I knew all the speed traps by heart, and turned down a more secluded junction off the main freeway, only one lane out, one way in. Harder to tail someone here.

This is what I did for the next couple of hours: drive around with no destination, in particular. I saw a drive-in diner, and pulled into the parking lot. I was parked front-out, when it was supposed to be front-in only. However, the spot was between two light posts, so I could sit in the dark and watch the hovertraffic.

As I continued to stare, I noticed a neon sign in the distance, and another, then more. All of them said, or were about the NeuroDancer.

I had left the offices, and driven into another part of the city. It was not unusual for me to meet a client off-site for the initial sit-down at a neutral place. Some people were more paranoid than I was, lately, and wanted to meet in public, or someplace secret. The Whisper Diner was both.

They had paid PJ a retainer in cash. The description of the person who came into the office to do that was different from the description of the potential client I was to meet. The only other thing we required was a phone number.

I sat outside in the Pony. The downpour was still heavy, and I watched the main entrance. All the other hovercars were parked in the back, except for one near the path to the front door.

I dialed the number. A man appeared on the screen of my mobile. "Mr. Jones?"

"Yes."

"Where are you?"

"I'm inside at the very back, sitting in the corner."

"Hold on," I got out of the Pony in the rain. I didn't use umbrellas. "Okay, I'm walking up to the diner. There's a hovercar parked in front of the door, and I'm walking past it—"

The hovercar exploded!

I flipped my mobile closed. I wasn't walking at all. I was pretending, and walking in place the whole time next to the Pony.

My impulse was to run inside to find the mutt, but I got close enough to the place to see the panic and commotion inside the diner, as the man bolted out of the back. I ran back to the Pony and jumped in. I knew the area, but could I catch him? Probably not. I had no idea what he was driving, or if any of the many hovercars leaving the scene from the back were him.

I watched the burning wreck. The fire was so intense that the rain wasn't going to put it out. I was going to call 9-1-1, but I was in no mood. I pulled out of there in the Pony for my office. Someone else would have to call.

CHAPTER 40

Punch Judy

I had never yelled at PJ before. I never yelled at anyone, except for criminals and criminal types. Yet that was what I did when I returned to the office. I'm sure everyone in the building heard me, I was so enraged.

A woman on the way up in the elevator, seeing my face, asked me, "Are you okay, sir?"

"I'm tired of people trying to kill me, and I'm going to end it!" I snapped at her.

The woman ran away as if she were on fire when the elevator door opened.

"No more, PJ!" I yelled. "There was a bomb in the hovercar!"

She said nothing as I stormed into my private office. I sat down at my desk to calm myself. I heard the vid-phone.

"Who are you calling?" I yelled.

No answer, but I could hear the whispering. I was about to march back out there, when she appeared at the open doorway.

"Did you call the police?" she asked.

"No." I sat back down. "There's a diner full of people there. Let them call the police."

"I have that man on surveillance tape. I'll find out who he is." She disappeared to her desk.

"You do that!"

I didn't want to work. I didn't want to do anything. I placed my head down on my desk to take a nap.

CHAPTER 41

Tuck Rogers and Perfect Tony

There was a knock at the door.

I felt as if I were recovering from a hangover, but I hadn't had anything to drink. At my open door was Tuck Rogers.

"Mr. Cruz, I hear you need some cheering up."

It was the same set-up as last time, Tuck in the passenger seat, Perfect Tony in the back.

"It reminds me of one of my earlier roles," Tuck began. "I was a fresh new kid on the set. I think it was my first movie where my name wasn't buried in the end credits somewhere. This was maybe 30 years ago. I had just gotten my contract with the studio. I was walking on clouds. I played this secret agent, and the director wanted to keep everything really gritty, raw, in your face. So, he had me skip rehearsals. He didn't even want me to meet the actor who played the criminal who was going to try to kill me. We were going to spend one whole day, one long day, with only this sequence. No guns or weapons. It was going to be a medieval fight to the death with bare hands. My character knocked his laser gun out of his hands, and he tried to get mine, but in the struggle, I kicked it over the side of a cliff. It fell hundreds of feet off the side. Our characters then faced off, with only our hands as weapons. He had to kill me, because he was the bad guy. I had to kill him, because he had killed my partner in a horrific spaceship battle. Only one man was going to be coming out of this alive.

"The filming was brutal: wide shots, birds-eye view, ground view, but the close-ups—strangling, gouging out eyes, trying to rip a man apart. It was the most brutal sequence I ever did in my career. The end product made everyone cringe, but when it was released, audiences loved it. I got all kinds of awards for it. I never did anything as graphic ever again, but I always remembered it. It was one of those defining roles that put you on the map. All my roles since then have been popcorn, pop culture, space swashbuckler fluff. It's made me a space barge full of money, but it was that role, out of all my many movies, that I remember the most."

"Tuck, that scene of yours is one we still study in acting college," Perfect Tony added. "I saw that movie, and that's when I said I wanted to be an actor for life. It was the only thing I ever wanted to do after seeing that."

"Thanks for that, Perfect T.," Tuck said. "It's good when your life can be an inspiration to the next generation. How do you do it, Mr. Cruz?" Tuck asked me.

"Yeah, Cruz. How do you process that? Another person trying to take your life in real life."

"It comes with the job," I answered. "It used to bother me a lot before, but I realized this was work that I was good at, and this was the price.

"When I was starting out, I had a posthumous mentor. His name was Wilford G. He died at 92, and was a private detective in Metropolis for 70 years—talk about seeing it all. He did, and more. He wrote a book called *How to be a Great Detective with 100 Rules*. In it, he had so many witty sayings, but the advice—it was what helped me more than anything else. He never got hysterical or upset, never was fearful about the danger. He simply said that being a good detective in this city was a blessing and that danger was the price of membership. Protect yourself, but it's all part of the life."

"He was a wise man," Tuck said.

"He must have been. His son is a Metro police sergeant, and head of their union. I've met him, and he's a solid guy, too. Too bad I never got to meet Wilford G. in real life. Now, there's a guy you two should have had the chance to do a ride-along with—the stories he could tell you."

"Mr. Cruz, his stories would have been unforgettable, undoubtedly." Tuck casually reached over and touched the right side of my steering wheel, which seemed strange.

I glanced at him for only a second. When I did, I yelled, but no sound came out. The pain was so intense; I felt my entire body being pulled up, out of the driver's seat, into the back. With my feet off the pedals, the Pony went into stall mode. Tuck pulled my body out of the driver's seat, as he threw his body into the driver's seat and took control. My eyes were shut, my body was shaking, I was passing out.

Pop!

My pop-gun fired, snapped the cord crushing my neck, and blew a hole through the top of the Pony.

My eyes opened. Tuck's fist caught me in the face; my head slammed against the passenger window. I yelled out like a madman, lifted my legs, and started kicking him as wildly as I was screaming.

I noticed Pretty Tony lunging at me from the back. I fired the pop-gun again; he anticipated my move, and ducked down. The blast blew out my rear window. While still kicking Tuck, him blocking as many of the kicks as possible, I hit a lever with my gun hand. My driver's door blew out, and I threw my body towards the driver's seat as I kicked out with my legs.

"Ahh!" Tuck stopped blocking, as he gripped the steering wheel, but too late. I kicked Tuck Rogers out of the Pony. All I heard were his screams, then a horrific thud, then a crash, then a series of crashes. We were 30 feet in the air!

Where was Perfect Tony?

The fear was almost shaking my body apart. The other actor wasn't in the Pony. I heard footsteps outside, on the top of the vehicle. I got fully into the driver's seat, and pulled the vehicle to the closest pit-stop, on the closest rooftop.

I had no more pellets in the pop-gun, and frantically looked around. I wasn't paying attention. The Pony crashed into the roof's surface. I powered it off. Perfect Tony jumped down from the top of my vehicle to the driver's side, and snatched me out of the Pony.

It was his turn at the kick-the-human-to-death game. With rain and blood in my eyes, I couldn't see. Perfect Tony knew how to kick perfectly. I couldn't move at all; the kicks to my body were so savage. He stopped. I opened my eyes, at first didn't see him, then noticed him flying down from the air at me. I rolled away. He tried to jump on my head. I decided it was the only thing I could do, so I started rolling and rolling away from the roof edge—and him.

"I'm going to stomp your brains out. Keep rolling, because when you can't roll any further, that's when I begin." Perfect Tony was Psycho Tony.

I wasn't able to roll any further. I'd reached the wall of the elevator banks. I tried to shoot the pop-gun at him in desperation, but it was futile. As I watched him walk closer, I felt everything about this was all wrong. I was not at 100%. I wasn't fighting. What was wrong with me?

I made the decision. I was not dying like this! I crawled up, and then got to my feet to face him. He marched toward me like an advancing killer robot. I had no idea what I was going to do. I had to get crazy and mentally prepared. Engage my inner OCD to the task at hand. He hits you once, you hit him 50 times. Do beyond what is possible.

Perfect Tony drew a gun that I didn't know he had, and pointed it at me. "Principal photography begins on my next movie tomorrow, so I can't have you marking up my face."

A hovercar bug came from nowhere and smashed Perfect Tony into the elevator banks. I instinctively got out of the way, falling to my feet. I stared at his broken body on the ground. Perfect Tony, too, would not be doing anymore movies in his life, ever again.

I looked up as I heard the hovercar driver's door open. It was Dot!

My mouth hung open as I watched the wife walk to me. Her face was flushed with distress. She looked at Perfect Tony's dead body, and then looked at me.

"I'm sorry, Cruz. I didn't mean to kill him. It was supposed to be a slight bump. Did you need to interrogate him?"

CHAPTER 42

SAG

My Pops told me the secret to a long and happy marriage was, when the wife asked a question, know whether to answer it, or change the subject. My wife and I had killed two of the planet's leading movie stars. My wife and I had cost, and would cost, the major studios who knows how many billions in lost revenue.

I didn't care!

"Give me your mobile," I said to my wife.

She fished it out of her pants pocket. It was hot pink, of course, and I opened it.

"Are you calling the police?"

"No," I snapped. I dialed. PJ answered. "PJ, who was the person who set up the ride-along with the movie actors?"

"Her name's Sheer, with an S."

"Which studio is she with?"

"She's not with the studio. Her office is at the Screen Actors Guild at—"

"I know where it is." I hung up the line.

I handed the mobile back to the wife.

"Cruz, what's happening?"

"Call the police, and wait for them. You won't have to wait long, because with all of this, they're probably already here. I have to go. Tell them I'll personally stop by Police One, but I have to do something."

"Cruz! You can't leave."

"Stay here and wait."

"Where are you going?"

"First, it was accountants; now actors are trying to kill me. I'm getting to the bottom of all this, once and for all."

My wife called after me, but I got into the one working elevator capsule. The first person I saw, I gave a few bucks to call me a hovercab. It arrived, and I was off to SAG.

The Screen Actors Guild headquarters of Metropolis was in Paisley Parish—the same town as Eye Candy. The tower was designed to look like three beams of light coming out of a huge strobe light pointed into the sky. I must have looked the way I felt—beaten, broken, and ready to fall over, based on the expressions of the lobby doormen.

"Where's Mrs. Sheer's office?" I asked them.

"Are you okay, sir? Do you need medical attention?"

"What floor is she on? Never mind. What does Mrs. Sheer do for SAG?"

"Do, sir?" The doormen seemed puzzled by my question. "Ms. Sheer is the legendary casting director and a senior SAG board member."

They had a neon directory on the wall; I recognized her last name, and saw the floor number. I got on the elevator and went up.

When the door opened, I expected to see someone waiting for me, but there was no one. I got to the office number, and entered. Inside, people were all glued to the tv screens. It was on the news: the deaths of Tucker Rogers and Perfect Tony. People were in shock and crying.

I noticed pictures of people on the wall. The one that got my attention was of a man. I walked to it, and read the caption the name. Past treasurer? It was the second mutt on the case, who'd tried to kill me; I had nicknamed him "Rogue Two." I turned. No one in the office had even noticed I'd entered. They were all zombies, watching the television.

"Ms. Sheer!" I yelled.

She turned. Now, everyone in the office was watching me.

"You're through!" I yelled. "I know what you all did, and I'm going to tell everyone!"

"No," she pleaded. "Don't do that."

"You're through!"

"Please. We can work it out. Anything you want. Whatever price. Name it. We can work it out. Money, women, any actress you want, anything you want."

I was so disgusted. I stormed out of the office.

The door hadn't even closed when people from the office ran after me. I was too weak to do anything, as they all jumped me!

"Get off me!"

They had me pinned down to the ground.

"What do we do?" a man asked.

All of them, I could see it in their faces, were distressed, desperate.

"We have to do something," he said.

"Get off me! The police are on the way! It's over!" I yelled out, with a dozen sitting on top of me.

"Kill him," Ms. Sheer said. "It's all we can do. Dispose of the body before they get here."

"What!" I yelled. "Are you crazy?"

These were amateurs, but dangerous amateurs could be as deadly as any professional. They lifted me up to my feet; that's when I pushed them and broke free. I tried to run, but they tackled me. They tried to pin me to the ground again, and I saw more people running down the hall at me. These new guys were real thugs, not office workers. Ms. Sheer just pointed them to me. The office people were replaced by the basement thugs. The men were big, muscular, and menacing. I couldn't break free from them.

"Hey! What are you doing?"

We all looked towards the voice. None of them knew who the men were, but I did. It was the Hovertruckers Union boss, and his men that Dot and I had met with.

"Why don't you let, Mr. Cruz go?" the boss said.

"Why don't you get out of here? You're trespassing," one of the SAG thugs yelled.

"Are we supposed to be scared?" a Hovertrucker thug asked, as they laughed.

"Mr. Bar, are sure you want to do this?" It was a new voice. It came from a SAG thug-in-a-suit. "If you don't take your men off this floor and out of this building, I'm going to make one call. By the end of the hour, every major studio in Metropolis will cancel every contract with the Hovertruckers Union, and boycott any future work, or anyone who does business with your union."

Bar and his men lost their menace. They looked like a bunch of mice, all of a sudden.

"Bar," I yelled, "they're going to kill me because I stumbled on their plot to replace all dock and transportation jobs with robots from Up-Top!" Yes, I could spontaneously lie better than most.

That did it. I got two key words in before the SAG people stifled me: robots and Up-Top. Earth unions hated both, and I found myself in the middle of an all-out brawl. I was completely useless, but I did manage to trip one SAG person, and smack another in the nose. The Hovertrucker Union thugs were a force of destruction, and not even the SAG union thugs could stop them.

Then, SAG security swarmed out of the elevators, and subdued everyone. We were all on our knees, with our arms handcuffed behind our backs.

Ms. Sheer was whispering to one of the SAG guards, and I knew the badness was far from over. The SAG guard looked at me, and then started my way. Five feet away, he began to draw his weapon.

"Oh, no you don't!" I leapt up and rushed him.

I wasn't alone. The other Hovertrucker Union guys had done the same; we rammed the security guards, and knocked them down. All the SAG security guards drew weapons.

"This is the police! Everyone drop your weapons, or be fired on and killed!"

The spotlights beamed through the glass hallway windows at either end, as the directives rumbled through. The SAG security guards froze, not knowing what to do.

"If you morons don't drop your weapons now, they're going to machine-gun you through the glass!" I yelled.

The SAG security guards began to throw their guns to the ground. Elevators beeped, and silver-and-black Metro police swarmed in.

I closed my eyes, sighed, and allowed my body to fall to the ground, to relax.

The police moved all of us to the building tower lobby. They arrested everyone—me, the Hovertrucker Union guys, all SAG employees, including security, even the mailman who'd had the misfortune of being on the floor at the time. We were all sitting on the ground in different groups, with our hands handcuffed behind our backs, with a few police officers watching us all.

Outside the ground floor windows of the tower seemed to be the entire world. The police had it all cordoned off, and people behind the barricade, but the flash of cameras from the ground and media hovercraft was blinding.

We heard commotion, and a man was let in, but with all the bright lights, I couldn't quite make out who it was.

An officer approached me. "Mr. Cruz."

"Yes," I answered.

"Your lawyer is here. You're so big now, that you need a lawyer."

"I didn't call any lawyer."

"So big that you don't even need to call your lawyer."

He let me get to my feet, and follow him to a quiet section of the lobby. It was Mr. Meta! The man came close, and I couldn't help staring. The larger-than-life studio head looked as if he'd been crying all day. His eyes were red, his hair unkempt.

"Mr. Meta, what's wrong?"

"Tell me what you want. I'll give you anything to keep it quiet. It's not about the money for me. It's about my legacy. My life's work. Tell me what you want, and I'll give it to you," he begged. "Anything at all. Anything."

I said nothing. There was nothing to say. They were all terrified of me—terrified of something they thought I knew. I would find out what it was, eventually. I always did. But to watch such powerful people fall to pieces in front of me—they'd sell their souls, to keep me from finding out their secret.

Mr. Meta was mumbling to himself. He shuffled away, and out of the building's main entrance.

However, I didn't know what the secret was yet.

I walked over to the officer who had been watching us.

"Officer, could I ask one of my colleagues for their mobile phone to make a call?" I asked.

"You can ask, but I'm not unhandcuffing you."

"Why not? They were trying to kill me."

"We have your wife in custody, too."

The statement made me stop.

"Throwing a person out of a moving hovercar, Mr. Cruz, is a murder."

"He—was trying to kill me."

"Running down a human being with a hovercar and killing them is murder, Mr. Cruz."

I was started to get mad.

"Where did your lawyer go? You really do need that person for where you're going."

"I'm innocent. They tried to kill me."

"The story of your life, Mr. Cruz."

CHAPTER 43

Bite-Size

It was one thing for me to be in trouble, but now, my wife had been arrested.

The officer had me sitting back with my group of hovertruckers, but I was fuming mad, restless, irritable, unable to sit still.

"Mr. Cruz, if you don't calm down, they're going to stun you," Bar said.

"They arrested my wife!"

"Cruz, I feel for ya, but you gotta calm down. You're not helping yourself, and you're not helping her, by working yourself up."

"I need to make a call. I can't just sit here."

"Here comes one of the cops," one of the hovertrucker thugs said.

We looked to see another officer approaching. "Okay, Cruz, get to your feet. You're getting the special treatment, your own personal shuttle back to Central."

"I want to go back with everyone else."

"That hurts, Cruz. We thought you were a friend of law enforcement. How could you hurt our feelings like that?"

"I want to stay with everyone else, and go back with them."

"Yeah, let him go back with us," Bar said.

"Cruz, Cruz, Cruz." It was Officer Break with his partner Caps walking to us. "We go on a short vacation, and you're up to your old tricks again."

"He doesn't want to go with us," the other police officer said.

"Cruz is finicky, like a cat. He has to get to know you, before he warms up to you. Cruz, come on. Let's go."

I stayed quiet in the hovercruiser ride to Police Central. Even Officer Break, who was always chatty said nothing. That worried me.

"When we get in, I want to see my wife." That was all I said.

I was in the interrogation box, still handcuffed, after an hour. They ignored me when I asked to see my wife and did the same when I asked for access to a phone. I had resorted to banging my forehead on the table periodically. I was moving to a state beyond stir-crazy.

The Organized Crime men entered the room.

"You're in so much trouble, Cruz."

"I need your mobile."

"Cruz, you're not getting a phone. You're being arrested."

"Give me a phone now, or I won't tell you how organized crime has infiltrated every major movie studio in Metropolis."

I realized I had gotten so good at making up lies, that sometimes I even believed them. The two OC men looked at each other and one of them put his mobile phone on the table; the other unhandcuffed me.

I grabbed the phone, and couldn't dial fast enough.

"Cruz!" It was Bite-Size's face on the screen. "I've been trying to find you."

"The only question I have is, do you know what this is about?"

"Cruz, it's big. It's bigger than big."

"I am about to be arrested, and have my life, and my wife's, turned into hell. If you get here, all that will be avoided, and you'll be able to buy that new hovercar you've had your eye on for years."

"Will you teach me to drive too—a real defensive driver?"

"Yes."

"I'm on my way to save the day, Cruz!"

CHAPTER 44

The Oldest Man on Earth

When they said he was the Oldest Man on Earth, I believed it. The man looked ancient. He walked into my interrogation room at sub-light speed (meaning he walked so damn slow it took him forever).

"Who are you?" I asked, with the OC men watching. A police officer led him inside.

The door opened again, and this time, it was a bunch of suits. I knew exactly who they were. They were the "booking crew." I was about to be booked, and formally charged. Even if I exonerated myself in court, which I knew I would, the fact was, that I would have been arrested. I'd never be able to say I'd never been for the rest of my life, and could never check "no" on any form again in the future. There would be jobs I could never take, and places I could never go, because I had been arrested for a crime, and a crime as serious as murder.

The OC men held up a hand, and the booking crew stood in the corner. Also entering the room was Chief of Police Hub. He stood quietly. I had escaped the very same thing in my last case (and probably *wouldn't* have been able to exonerate myself), and here I was in the same place again.

"Are you really the oldest man on earth?" I asked.

"No, no. It's the name of my cyber-site. Never heard of it?"

"No," I answered. "Why are you here?"

"Bite-Size sent me."

"I just hung up with Bite-Size, so it couldn't be him."

"He sent me here when you were still at SAG headquarters. Here, sonny."

The old man took out his own mobile, and set it on the table. He fiddled with it until he could play a video message.

"Cruz, this is Bite-Size. Obviously, it's Bite-Size, me. The Oldest Man on Earth is my business partner. I'm the youth, and he's the brains. When you've watched as many movies as I have, you know the guy who *isn't* the main protagonist, who knows the motive behind the crime, is always the one to get killed. That means me, so I'm sending Old Man, because no one knows him, and you never spoke to him, which makes him safe. I'm hiding out in a secret bunker until this all blows over. No criminals are going to get me. See you, Cruz. I don't know how you got into this case, but it's a doozy."

The video message cut off.

"Old Man, I'm running out of patience. What is this all about? Why did two studio accountants, two movie stars, a SAG board member, and an entire floor at the SAG headquarters try to kill me?" I asked.

I could see the booking crew looking at each other. Hub and the OC men were looking at each other too.

"Can I sit, sonny?"

One of the OC men helped him to a seat. Once seated, he leaned back, sighed, and smiled.

"How on earth did you stumble on this?"

"Stumble on what?"

"You don't even know."

"I'm not a big movie person so, no, I don't know. Why have they been trying to kill me? Why are they so scared?"

"Because you're about to kill Movie-Town, Mr. Cruz."

"What are you talking about?"

"Are you sure that's what you want to do?"

"Seeing as I'm about to get booked for murders, yes, let's do it. I'm not playing games. They've got my wife, too, you know."

"Oh yes, the woman on the rooftop. I saw that on the news. That's a shame. You don't want family involved in these things." He leaned forward. "It's all fake."

I looked at him. "What's fake?"

"The movie business."

"Yes, we all know that."

He shook his head. "You don't understand." He picked up his mobile phone and went to the Net. He found what he wanted. "Have you ever seen this movie?" He showed me the screen.

I leaned down to see the screen. "Yeah, I think so."

"When was it made?"

"I don't know. Over 10 years ago."

"What if I were to tell you it was made centuries ago?"

"Centuries ago?"

"Yes."

"That doesn't make any sense. Everything's different now compared to back then—fashion, vehicles, places."

"So is our technology. Take an old movie of yesteryear, run it through the studio's high-speed CGI programs of today, keep the actors, alter everything else. Besides key people in the media, at publicity firms, the awards shows, etc., no one on the outside would ever know—and they all get filthy rich."

"How many movies are we talking?"

"Hundreds, maybe thousands."

I was annoyed. "I still don't understand. The studios were releasing movies that were first made eons ago. Who cares? Re-releasing movies isn't illegal."

"Mr. Cruz, you seem a bit agitated. Bite-Size says you figure out things fast, but you did say your wife is in police custody, too, so I'll simply tell you.

"Re-releasing old movies isn't illegal, but that's not what the studios were doing. If you re-release an ancient movie, you pay a few fees here and there, and that's it. However, these were released as *new* movies. Investors financed budgets for actor salaries, director salaries, producer salaries—all that above-the-line talent has been dead a long time. So where has all that money been going? Actors also get residuals. Talent wins awards with money attached. Studios get the huge profits, including syndication and licensing. Where is all the money going? The studios have been presenting people as alive and kicking, pretending all these people, actors, directors, producers were alive today, when they've been dead, before there even was a Metropolis. They've been trying to kill you, Cruz, because you're about to crash a multi-trillion-dollar empire, and a whole lot of people are about to go to jail.

"How would you feel, as an investor, if you paid a quarter billion dollars to make a new movie when, in fact, it was an ancient movie, worth 50 bucks, made centuries ago, sitting in someone's film vault, and CGI'd to swindle you?"

"The Movie-Town Conspiracy Case—and everyone is involved. Okay, now I get the money part—and the motive, but what laws were broken?" I asked, looking up at Chief Hub, "besides the obvious multiple counts of attempted murder."

"Every kind of corporate fraud there is, tax evasion, misappropriation of funds, racketeering, identity theft, for starters," Hub said. "All felonies, by the way. If what you say is true, then, yes, we'll also be able to add attempted murder, conspiracy to commit murder, soliciting murder, and probably be able to squeeze in about a dozen other charges. They'll never see the light of day outside a prison ever again. After us, all those investors—the civil courts will get their pounds of flesh, with charges of their own."

The Old Man looked at me, smiling. "If I were them, I would have done everything possible in the world to kill you, too."

CHAPTER 45

Chief Hub

Mr. Meta was dead.

I heard he'd committed suicide. I was almost crying. I liked him, but as I sat in another, more comfortable waiting room, I realized I was as responsible for killing him as he was. I suspected that a large percentage of the movies he'd "made" and was known for worldwide, were, in fact, made by movie-makers centuries before any of us were born. He'd just found a way to appropriate them as his own, becoming super-wealthy and powerful as a result of his crime. He was a crook, but I still felt awful, remembering the last time I'd seen him mumbling and bumbling around. I'd watched the man watch his entire life crumble before his own eyes.

I was free. The booking crew had disappeared. I was unhandcuffed, and could make any calls I wanted—but I couldn't leave. My wife had been released two hours ago, so that was a relief.

An officer came and led me to Hub's office. In the room was the Mayor, and his chief aide. There were also other police brass, and the two OC agents. They acknowledged that I had entered, but they were all watching the news on the television screens on the wall.

The news had exploded. The frenzy of people being arrested was even too much for the sensationalist media—accountants, attorneys, assistants, casting directors, location directors, actors, directors, producers, studio chiefs, even other reporters. It was a conspiracy to make the world think hundreds of people were flesh and blood today, when they were long since dead. So many people had been making so much money for so long.

"The cover story," Hub said, looking at me directly, "is that organized crime took over elements of the movie business, and most of this was their work."

"Why would we say that?" I asked.

"Because, Mr. Cruz," the Mayor interjected, "after the movie industry in our supercity crashes and burns, it will need to be rebuilt. It only accounts for 40 percent of our economy. I apologize for looking at the bigger picture, but it will be easier for the public to embrace them again, if we can point to bad elements within the industry, rather than the industry itself."

"Sounds as if you have it all figured out, Mr. Mayor. Just make sure the actors and studio accountants that you get to replace this bunch don't ever try to kill me too. Or else I'll kick them out of my vehicle, or have my wife run them over with hers again. Anything else?"

"No, Mr. Cruz." The Mayor was disgusted by me, which was normal.

"I can finally go home and see my wife."

CHAPTER 46

Caret

Why did I answer the phone? I was so angry. I had just bought the new mobile. I had no idea where my old one was. With all that I'd been through, it could have been anywhere.

"Mr. Caret, what do you want?"

"Mr. Cruz, you've been a very busy person today. One of the producers I was going to make my movie with has been arrested, another has committed suicide, and the police are looking for me. You've cost me a lot of money, Mr. Cruz. More money than you could ever imagine."

"Have you and Logo killed each other yet?"

"You are a very annoying person, Mr. Cruz. I guess the joke is on me, for hiring you to begin with."

"Yes. Joke's on you. Ha-ha. Bye."

I hung up on him.

CHAPTER 47

Madness

The reason I was so mad, was that Dot had disappeared too. I had been speeding to my Liquid Cool office, when a video-call came in again. It was Caret's number.

Caret, you bastard, leave me alone! I answered the call.

I had used jetpacks before, but the straps on this one were so tight. It was practically crushing my chest. I knew I was on the roof of my building, one of the few times it wasn't raining. I stood on the very ledge of the roof, balancing, as I took off the jetpack.

As I got it off, finally, I fell forward. I didn't know what was happening. I fell and then felt something grab my ankles. My body was dragged up along the side of the building; I winced in pain. I was on the roof, and then someone lifted me off the ground. It was PJ. She held me in the air with my feet dangling off the ground. She was yelling to someone else, but I heard no words.

I saw The Mick, Run-Time's third VP, appear, and go behind me. I felt my arms being restrained. What were they doing to me? I didn't know what was happening.

Before I knew it, I was in the elevator. There was Phishy! Phishy was there too, holding the elevator when we got on, and when we got off. He opened the Liquid Cool office, and PJ carried me into my office.

There were Bugs, Run-Time, and Dot! What was happening? I didn't know what was happening. They all put me in this metal frame restraint.

"What are you doing to me?" I kept yelling. I tried everything, using all my might to break free, but I was trapped. I couldn't move my hands or my feet.

"Help me! Let me go!" I yelled.

Then they all left me in the room and closed the door.

I tried to shake my body free several times. I kept screaming, but it was hopeless. After, it seemed liked hours, I was tired. I calmed down.

That's when the door opened. The restraint they had me in was some type of chair. Dot knelt down to face me. I shook my head as I closed my eyes. She was talking, but I heard no words.

"Cruz, can you hear me?"

I opened my eyes. I could hear. "What are you doing to me?"

"Cruz, I'm going to ask you a question."

"What?"

"What were you doing on the roof?"

"I was looking around."

"For what?"

"I can't remember. I was looking around."

"Is that it?"

"Then you all attacked me. Why are you doing this?"

"Cruz, I want you to look at this."

She showed me a video replay. I watched myself exit the rooftop door, with a jetpack on. I powered it up, flew up in the air, and then landed on the ledge. I almost fell off, but managed to regain my balance. Then, inexplicably, I unfastened the straps, and threw the jetpack off the roof. As I let myself begin to fall off the roof, that's when PJ and The Mick burst out of the rooftop door. PJ didn't have bionic legs, but she ran so fast, it looked as if she did. While she grabbed my ankle with one hand, a projectile shot out of some weapon The Mick had, and attached to my back. I think it was a remote-controlled parachute. PJ dragged me up, back onto the roof, and away from the ledge.

"Cruz, why were you on the roof?" Dot asked me again.

"I was looking around—Let me go! Let me out of this restraint!"

I was becoming hysterical, but the wife remained calm.

"I'll let you go right now if—"

"Let me go!"

"If you answer one question for me, I'll let you go."

I stared at her.

"Answer one question; I'll let you go. Okay?"

"Let me go."

"Will you answer my question?"

"Yes," I answered after a long pause.

Dot began to release all the restraint bars. I had my hands free, and then my feet.

"Cruz, that day you left the offices for our wedding, the NeuroDancer came to the offices, and hired you."

I rubbed my wrists and hands after I pushed the chest restraint bar off of me. "Yes."

"What did she hire you for?"

Dot folded her arms, and waited for my answer.

My eyes darted around. I vividly remembered not wanting to take her case, then seeing all that money, and changing my mind. I told her she had hired herself a detective. I remember driving the Pony away from the offices, getting the traffic ticket, going to Good Kosher, then the

Concrete Mama. I could remember everything, but I couldn't remember anything in the office after I took her case. Nothing. I tried so hard to remember.

I finally looked at Dot. I angrily yelled, "She did something to me!"

I grabbed my fedora off my head, threw it across my office, and marched to my couch. I threw myself onto it, with my back facing out, my hands tucked between my legs.

I was done! I was done with private investigation! I was done with Liquid Cool! I was done with it all!

PART SIX

Prime Numbers

CHAPTER 48

China Doll: The Chronicle of the Wife

Cruz was done!

It was more than a juvenile tantrum. It meant he wasn't talking or engaging with anyone for hours. When that was done, he'd storm off to his vehicle to drive home, and do the same thing for days or weeks on end. His mother told me he'd done it a few times, growing up. I'd never seen it before, but every time around his birthday, he'd disappear to be alone—a trait I was going to remedy him of now that we were married—but this was serious.

He threw his fedora across the room on the floor. Cruz was a borderline germophobe. First, that was his lucky hat. He treated that hat the same way he treated his classic hovercar—with white glove care, at all times.

Second, he threw it on the floor. Cruz didn't put anything on the floor. Even his shoes when he got home were on a special anti-bacterial heating rack. I did catch him lying on the floor of the Liquid Cool office when he first got it, but normally, the floor, the ground, except for at the

Centers for Disease Control, was a no-no. You didn't put anything on the floor, and anything that fell on it was bound for the trash chute.

Third, Cruz wore the lucky hat all day. Once he put it on for the day, it wasn't coming off for any reason, all day, until he got home and it was bed time. Many people didn't know it, but he'd made a secret see-through strap for it, that he'd fasten under his chin, sometimes, so the wind couldn't blow it off. That hat stayed on. He didn't have just the one. He had several, and when he wasn't wearing the others, he had some kind of weird steaming, anti-germ, anti-whatever-contaminant mini-chamber that he kept them in that I think he got from somewhere. Maybe it was the CDC too. The hat thing was a big deal.

Also, he was on the couch with his back outward. I glanced over, and could see his eyes weren't closed. This was very, very bad. It meant he was not mad; he was psycho-mad. In his mind, he was focused completely on the thing or person who'd upset him. If there'd been such a thing as pyro-telekinesis, and he'd had it, they'd be burning up in a big bonfire that very moment. When Cruz locked in on you, there was no escape. So many people had found out what a fully-engaged OCD person could do when one focused in on you.

I remember the poor man who'd scratched Cruz's hovercar. Well, he wasn't poor, maybe working class, and he was a big jerk, so he deserved it. Cruz stalked him to the ends of the Earth, until he paid the money to fix the car. It wasn't stalking like 9-to-5. It was stalking 24/7. That man was so scared at the end, he'd have paid anything to make Cruz go away. Clearly, I had only learned of this story after we'd been dating a long while. I wondered if NeuroDancer were burning up now in a hotel room or hoverlimo somewhere.

Then there was the yelling. Cruz didn't yell at friends or family. He yelled at strangers, and what he called mutts—punks. Cruz had a very precise code of behavior in life: how he dressed, how he talked. A hovercar of a certain vintage wasn't a car; it was a vehicle. Cops weren't "cops," unless they worked for traffic or parking enforcement. He only used the word "police." He never used degrading words about women (that's one I couldn't say I did), no ethnic slurs, didn't do ethnic jokes, did do the demeaning jokes about off-worlders though, but all Earth people did that, and they had jokes about us. Cruz lived by this code. Run-Time called it his coolness. I called it "Cruz control." Well, the yelling proved he wasn't himself.

Cruz had work to do. He couldn't be in this state for days, weeks, or months. That bitch did something to my husband, and none of us could figure out how. That meant she could do it again.

We left the door open; PJ and I watched him from the reception area.

"What do we do now?" PJ asked.

I looked at The Mick, who was standing. Run-Time, Phishy, and Bugs were all sitting in the lobby chairs. "Could you stay in there and watch him?"

The Mick nodded, and walked into the office. Phishy followed him.

I looked at PJ sadly. "Do we have anything at all?"

PJ shook her head.

"Run-Time, how is she doing it?"

Bugs stood up. "Whatever the method is, it's not mechanical."

"It's not any kind of drugs, either," Run-Time said. "Doll, we've done every kind of test known to humankind."

"Hypnotism?" I asked.

"Hypnotism doesn't work like that," Run-Time answered. He put a reassuring hand on my shoulder. "We don't know how, but we're going to keep looking. In the meantime, we won't let him out of our sight."

"He was seconds from jumping off the roof of a building. How does someone do that?" I looked at Bugs. "You said he received a video-call."

"Yes," Bugs answered. "The call was not even 30 seconds."

"We can't watch him forever."

"We'll figure it out," Run-Time said.

"No," I said. "Cruz will figure it out. He probably already has. We just need to get him out of the state he's in."

I walked to PJ's desk and looked at the piles. "Where's the stuff on her?"

"Here." PJ opened the top folder of one of the files.

"When we were looking at the pictures before, we noticed all her backup dancers were female. It used to be mixed. Male dancers, too."

"What are you thinking?" Run-Time asked. "She doesn't have any male dancers anymore because she mind-controls men only?"

"Yes," PJ replied. "Maybe, too much mind-control makes them too crazy and uncontrollable."

"With a plausible theory, I can walk in there, and we can possibly snap him out of his state. Let's look through all of it again."

We took all the folders we had, plopped them down on the main lobby table, and all four of us went through the photos. We went through them fast, because we had been going through all this material for days.

I walked back into the office with PJ at my side. All I brought with me was the one folder, and I slowly walked to Cruz. The couch he was on was against the wall, but there a tiny space between them. I peeked over his shoulder, and his eyes were open in death-stare mode. I angled my body slightly into the space between the couch and the wall.

"Cruz, you need to go to work, and finish this case. The only case here is the NeuroDancer case; you need to solve it, and you need to get it solved now. We knew she did something to you back then, so we've been working the case too. I think we came up with something. We don't know what she did. We don't even know how to reverse it, but you've told me a million times, there's always a workaround.

"We went through all the photos of her performances. The climax of most of them is her dancing solo at the end, but for the warm-up and most of the show, she has a dance team with her. For years, the team had always been women and men. Then there weren't any men. PJ and I looked forever, tracking down her last male dancers. One committed suicide, another died of a drug overdose, others disappeared. We couldn't find anything on them. You'd think, if you danced with NeuroDancer, even one time, you'd be everywhere—not any of them—gone. So for the last good few years, her dancers have only been women, so no suicides or disappearing dancers anymore."

There it was!

Cruz's death stare was interrupted. I could see his eyes looking to the side.

Suddenly, he jumped up from the couch—even PJ was startled—and walked across the room. The other guys watched from the open doorway.

Cruz picked up his tan fedora from the floor, put it on his head, positioned it the way he always does, and looked at me with a smirk, his hands on his hips.

I smiled.

Cruz was back! "NeuroDancer, my husband is coming for ya!"

CHAPTER 49

The Peanut Gallery

"**M**y friends," I said.

We were all sitting in the lobby area, with files on the table.

"Cruz is back!" Phishy said, laughing in his Phishy way.

The front door was locked, and all incoming calls were forwarded to messages.

"Why didn't you tell me?" I asked.

"Because we weren't sure," Dot replied. "We knew something was wrong, but didn't know for sure. So, we watched you."

"No, something more tangible must have tipped you off."

"I went to the fashion show, and taped it," PJ answered.

"What?"

"You remember you gave me the ticket to the NeuroDancer show?"

"Yes, but you didn't go."

"I did go. You said you weren't going to go, but you did, too. I was on the balcony, and when she came in...I thought you were acting weird. So, I took out my mobile and taped it."

"Recorded the show."

"No. Recorded you watching the show."

"Cruz, you were not acting right," Dot said.

"Then I watched you. She hired you, and gave you all that money that day, but you were never working on a case. We waited for days, but you never were working on a case for her. Why did she come into the office, then? Free money is good, but she was up to something, and she did something to you," PJ said.

"Where's that recording?" I asked.

PJ handed me a mobile phone. She told me the date, and I found it. We all watched it, and even I was taken aback. It was the combination of a leery pervert, and hyper-hormonal teenager. It was not what I remembered at all. I remembered the show as basically being boring.

I stopped the recording, and looked at everyone.

I looked at Run-Time and The Mick. "Do you realize the implications of this?"

The Mick said, "It means one of the biggest performers on the planet knows how to mind-control men. There isn't a government, megacorporation, or criminal who wouldn't do anything in their power to get their hands on that power."

"Dot is right," I said.

"I am?" she asked.

"This is the NeuroDancer show. It's all her."

"One time, you said you were suspicious of Beta Max," PJ added.

"Oh, he's involved all right, but he's not the ultimate puppet-master. He may think he is."

I stood from my seat. "We have work to do. PJ."

"Yes." She stood up, too.

"Find me a photo, any photo, with Beta Max and her, together."

She smiled. "Already done." She ran to her desk, rifled through other folders and came with, not one, but several photos. "Here you go. They were married once."

"What?"

"Yes," Dot said. "Before NeuroDancer was a world-famous dancer, the b—" My wife stopped herself. "She was a stripper. Mr. Beta Max owned the club. They were married for a time."

"Divorced?"

"Yes."

"But we couldn't find any record of it," PJ added.

"So, they could still be married."

"She has a lot of boyfriends," Dot said derisively.

"Yeah, two of my other clients."

"Who?" both PJ and Dot asked.

"Mr. Caret and Mr. Logo."

The revelation caught everyone off-guard.

Dot smiled, and pointed to everyone. "See, I told you. Cruz is already figuring it all out."

"Phishy," I said.

"Yes!"

"I have two tasks for you."

"Two?"

"I can do some tasks," Dot said.

"Dot, you are going back to Eye Candy to work."

"What?"

"You have already done the ultimate task. You organized this intervention team. You got my butt off the couch." She laughed. "But that's it. Let's not forget we both were at Police Central, seconds from being booked for murder. How exactly would that call have gone to our parents? Hey, Ma, hey, Dad, we're married, and are so in love that we're even going to jail for murdering movie stars together—the honeymoon suite at Metro Federal Penitentiary. No, Dot. You've done your part already. This is dangerous, and now, you know that first-hand—unless you *like* running people down with your little hoverbug."

"No." She held up her hand. "Once is enough for me."

"Now, I know why you had me go to the Hovertruckers Union meeting with you. You're so sneaky."

"They were good bodyguards, weren't they?" she said.

"Hovertrucker thugs versus SAG thugs—SAG thugs get sent straight to the hospital every time. They were literally life savers."

"That's why we hired them. They also helped watch you."

"What do I do?" Phishy asked.

"PJ, open the office for business. Get through the messages, and bring in help, if needed. I have a feeling that one or more of those messages could be very important. Phishy, how many sidewalk sallies are in the Brigade?"

Phishy smiled. "I know what you want to do."

"Get them all here in the office, and then you get the next task."

"Run-Time, is there a major political firm that starts with the word Prime? Part of its company name."

"Prime Numbers." He gave me a look. "What about them?"

"Mr. Cruz, you've just destroyed Movie-Town—" The Mick scolded.

"I didn't destroy anything," I said. "They were doing illegal things, and they probably could've continued to do their illegal things for as long as they wanted, but they had to try to kill me, multiple times, using accountants as hitmen. We can't have that."

The Mick sighed. "No, we can't."

"Are you suggesting Prime Numbers is doing something illegal?" Run-Time asked me.

I looked dead at him. "She was involved with the movie biz, through Mr. Caret. I found out what she was up to. She called me on the Pony. Next thing you know, I'm about to do a header off the roof. She's involved with Prime Numbers somehow, through Mr. Logo, her other boyfriend. So let me find out what she's up to there—only no more trying to take a header off the roof."

"No, we can't have that," Run-Time said.

"Bugs," I said. "Do you have any theories as to how she could be doing this?"

The man shook his head. He had a pained look. "We tried everything."

"We've been at it since last week," Run-Time added.

"The only theory I can come up with is, she physically came into the office with you. What did she have with her?"

"The briefcase of money," I answered. "Maybe it was much more than a briefcase."

"Exactly. A device."

"Bugs, I need a monitor in my office, so PJ can keep an eye on me. Can you make me some kind of wrist panic-button, so if I ever feel muddled or confused, and I don't have anyone with me, I can use it?"

"We were going to suggest something similar."

"Great minds always think alike. While you all do your tasks, and Run-Time takes his employees back to his fancy building, I'm taking my wife back to work. We've got lots of bills to pay, so we need both paychecks."

CHAPTER 50

Wilford Jr.

I don't know why it still bothered me, but I was still a bit upset over Mr. Meta's suicide. Was I getting soft on crime? No, but I was adult enough to be able to distinguish between different crimes. There was illegal activity, and real crimes. I stopped myself. These movie people had sent accountants and actors after me. They were even pondering how to kill me in the hallway of their own offices! The studio mogul was part of the conspiracy money train, but was he part of the conspiracy to make me a permanent resident of the morgue? I might never know.

The fallout of the Movie-Town scandals was far from over. The media was calling them the Gangsters of SAG. People were still being arrested, and people were still committing suicide to escape arrest or ruin. That's what gave me pause. That meant broken homes and broken families. A mass of collateral damage to many, many innocent people. All these people had benefited, so they were involved, but that didn't necessarily mean they needed to suffer.

Bad things happened in Metropolis all the time, and I couldn't blame myself for it. Much of it would happen whether I turned left or right in the Pony, but I needed to remain aware of that which was a result of me. Good guys can cause bad things to happen, even when doing good.

Dot was safely in Eye Candy's care, and I returned to the office.

I walked in and there they were.

Phishy saw me, and did his chicken-dance greeting. When he danced himself out to the laughter of the lobby crowd, I could assess the new additions to the Sidewalk Brigade. There were many thousands of sidewalk johnnies in Metropolis, but there were also sidewalk sallies. Not as many, but a lot in the supercity. In my office was a bunch of them waiting. They were in their slickers and, probably due to Phishy being Phishy, were all wearing dark fedoras, just like the sidewalk johnnies in the Brigade.

Now, I could get out there and do some work!

Before we left, there was one important thing for me to do. I sat in my office, while the sidewalk sallies waited, and made some final modifications to my omega-gun. In my previous case (Blade Gunner), I had the "pleasure" of meeting its original owner, and found out it had some girly modifications that I made Phishy get rid of. I had the pop-gun on the right forearm, the omega-gun attached to the left one, and I got a third piece for my shoulder holster.

Wilfred G., Jr. was not only the son of my posthumous mentor, Wilford G. He was the young union boss for the Metropolis Police Union—one of the most powerful unions in the supercity—500,000 strong.

When I called his office to talk with him, they patched me directly to him. When I asked to meet him at my favorite eatery, the Wet Cabeza, he said he'd meet me there for lunch.

"You're not very popular with the street cops at the moment," Wilford, Jr. said to me as he ate another bite of his pie. "Off-duty work at the studios can make up 25 percent or more of a cop's take-home pay. All that work is gone, suspended, until all this blows over. The Council of Corporations are involved, too. They say the studios and the city were in the conspiracy together. They're suing."

I laughed. "The studios were part of the Council."

"Exactly, but they're doing it to save face. My Fed friends say this is going to cut through the government and the Council soon. It's the tip of the iceberg. More high-profile arrests are coming—all this, from the case of one private detective."

"It's not my fault. They were doing illegal stuff. They shouldn't have tried to kill me. If they hadn't, they'd be fine."

Wilford G., Jr. laughed. "Their fatal mistake, going after you. Do you know I worked the Tuck Rogers scene? Did you really kick him out of your vehicle? He must have been hit by at least five hovercars on the way down. It was a major sky lane pile-up. It's a miracle no one else was killed, besides that other actor on the building rooftop. My partner worked that scene. Perfect Tony was definitely not so perfect anymore. What are we having lunch for, Cruz? What's the next chapter of mayhem you have in store for Metropolis?"

"Could you tell me about a company called Prime Numbers?"

He went white. "Good God, no. Why are you investigating them?"

I stopped him. "I'm not investigating them. I'm looking at them. Let's just say I have an arch-villain nemesis. She was—"

"She? A woman?"

"Yes, a woman. She was at the center of the Movie-Town mess, and I believe she's up to something with this company, Prime Numbers. I have no proof whatsoever, but this nemesis of mine wouldn't be interested in the company for nothing."

"What do you think it is?"

"I have no idea, but I'm going to find out."

"Why are you telling me this?"

"Because I know they were the company you hired for your union elections."

"You know that, do you?"

"I do."

"Cruz, I've seen your work from the start, when you first started private eye-ing. It's never small ball with you. It's always big with you. Look what's happening with Movie-Town. Look at your last major case Up-Top, Blade Gunner. It's never small with you. Now, you tell me the premiere political company in Metropolis, that I hired to help me get elected head of the Metro PD Union, and every mayor, councilman, judge, and commissioner has used to get themselves elected since I was in diapers, may be shady."

"I'm not saying that. I'm saying I have no idea, but I'm going to be poking around. I'm having lunch with you, because I wanted you to know. Just for you."

"What if I'm a bad guy?"

"You're the most popular leader the union ever had. Even on the remotest chance there's something criminal with this company, it wouldn't matter. If another election were held right now, you'd win unanimously. You're doing a solid job. Everybody says that, even the ones who didn't support you last time."

"Thanks for that. But you'd better be very cautious about how you go about this. There are lots of people who wouldn't be so okay with what you're doing."

"I know."

"People are still being arrested, and bodies are still being bagged for the morgue over your Movie-Town case."

"I know."

"I hope you're wrong."

"I hope so too, but this nemesis of mine—I think she'll go down as one of the greatest villains of all time in Metropolis, and you know I've come across a lot of them."

"Cruz, don't write the last chapter yet on your arch-villainess. Many a cop and many a Fed has made the same mistake. It's not over, until they're in jail or dead. Until then, you're the one who can end up dead."

CHAPTER 51

The Chronicle of Jed

I had an arch-nemesis. She was not stupid. I had no doubt she knew her last stunt to have me dive off a building like a bird without wings had failed. I was going to assume she knew I was onto her. The Movie-Town mess would have been a big part of her scheme, so she wasn't about to let me mess with another. She was going to try to do something about it. Maybe it would be to come after me, but that's not the action of a feline criminal. She was going to try to cover her tracks, keep me from figuring out the big picture.

It was a race.

But as I thought about it, there were two different strategies at work. One was the canine criminal ways: trying to gun me down on the street, in the hallway of my office, garrote me (I had to look that up, because I'd forgotten the term) in my own Pony, the hovercar bomb. This all spoke of different people, each doing their own thing. It might have been part of her overall criminal plan, but she wasn't directing them. Her calling me—and I knew it was her—to make me go zombie and jump off the roof, was her. I realized the Rogue Two incident was her, but it wasn't to kill me, rather to cover her tracks.

What would make all this so difficult, was that I didn't have to contend with just her, but all the little minions running around. Yes, it was a race. The Movie-Town mess was going to make all of them accelerate their respective plots. All I had to do was watch, and wait for my opportunity to pick them off, one by one.

The House of Jed had its own silver and white limo for the Master. It was a mode of transportation he used frequently. Into the rain he went, with the driver, a bodyguard in the passenger seat, and him sitting in the back, staring out the window.

The hoverlimo set down in a dark alley, with the only light being a flickering street lamp about 15 feet away. Jed began to exit the limo.

"Master," the driver said to him, looking in the rearview window.

Jed stopped. "I'll be okay. Nothing can happen to any of us. The force of the universe protects all members of the House. Do as we planned and keep circling the block until I come out."

Jed got out, and the hoverlimo rose into the sky. Jed reached into his jacket for a laser gun, and put the weapon under his jacket in his back waistband instead. He turned, and went into the seedy Goliathan warehouse structure.

It would take him 15 minutes to get from one side to the other, where there was a light. When he appeared, there was a dark-skinned man waiting.

Jed sighed.

The man stood from his stool. "You recognize me."

"How are you?" Jed said.

"Well, look at you, all respectable and a big religious leader. To think, when we last saw each other, you were just some punk agent of evil."

"Flyboy, is it still?"

"Oh, it is, especially after the circumstances of our last meeting. Master Jed, is it?"

"All that was a long, long time ago."

"In a galaxy far, far away, or something like that."

"Did Caret send you?"

"Who's that?"

"Never mind."

"I'm sorry, Master Jed. Are you feeling a little vulnerable at the moment?"

"I'm here for a simple exchange. I have the cash, if you have the item."

"A helmet."

"The helmet."

"Why do you want it?"

"If you want me to answer questions, then you have to pay me."

Flyboy smiled. "I can understand that. What if I don't want to give you the helmet? You can get a hoverbike helmet in any store in the city. Why this one?"

"Sentimental value."

"Something of value hidden in it."

"Sentimental value."

"Master Jed, I have a confession. Your religious group hears confessions, right?"

"It does."

"I have a confession. Do you need to be a member of your religious house?"

"No, actually. We help all in need, whether they're members or not."

"Aww, how religious of you. My confession—Jed—is, I don't have the helmet. I never had the helmet. The only thing I've got for you is a bullet to the head. You religious types don't believe in guns, do you?"

"No, or carrying them. It's against our religion."

"Isn't that funny? Maybe you should have stayed a gangster, and you wouldn't be in this position."

"The force of the universe protects all members of the House of Jed."

Flyboy laughed. "Keep saying that to yourself."

He went for his weapon, but Jed already had his, and shot Flyboy in the face, dead. Jed dived to the ground, and it seemed as if a million laser blasts came at him all at once from the darkness.

"This is R-6 coming in."

"This is R-3 coming in."

"This is R-5 coming in."

"This is R-2 leader coming in."

The hoverlimos descended from the dark sky. The vehicles flew into the warehouse and hovered above the ground, low enough for white-robed "knights" to jump out. They ran to the fire-fight, as they shot their own laser rifles into the darkness at the erupting laser blasts. The laser blasts shifted to them as targets.

Jed lay on the ground in the dark, quietly waiting.

Another Jed hoverlimo flew over the warehouse, and launched something. The grenade crashed through the roof. The light grenade engaged, the darkness in the entire warehouse was gone, and the army of thugs firing their weapons was revealed.

Jed, with goggles on, leapt up from the pavement, and ran at the thugs. He no longer had his gun, but a small laser-tipped blade. He sliced through them, then jumped, kicked, dived, ducked, each time impaling, slicing, or decapitating another thug. Others were cut down by laser blasts from the approaching group of the white-robed knights. By the time they'd gotten to their Master, all the thugs were dead.

"We have to get out of here as quickly as possible!" He ran with them, back the way they had come.

Jed heard something drop in the corner, and instinctively tried to shield his people. The sonic blast blew all of them back in the direction they were running.

Half-conscious, he watched what seemed to be an army of thugs enter and march to him with the largest laser rifles he'd ever seen.

One of the men knelt on one knee, and laughed. "We're impressed. You still know how to fight. I guess, once an agent of evil, always an agent of evil. You're too dangerous to leave around, so we'll be sending you onto the next plane of consciousness."

"This is the police! Freeze where you are!"

The beauty of those words was, that no matter who the criminal was, it made them freeze. No matter how tough or dangerous the criminal was, it sent a shiver down their spine. Metro Police were a scary thing to Metro criminals.

They all looked around, and then noticed the laser dots on their bodies from laser sniper rifles.

"Drop your weapons, or you will be fired upon and killed!"

The voice was so menacing. The thugs dropped their weapons, and put their hands in the air. You couldn't win a shoot-out with Metro Police. Surrender, get booked, get bailed out, go on to your next crime. That was the procedure. There was no need to get killed over possession of illegal firearms. It wasn't worth it. Firing at police, and living, was an automatic life sentence.

The voice directed them to put nose to pavement, with their arms and legs in spread eagle fashion. They all complied.

My sidewalk sallies came out with ultra flashlights in hand. Keeping the beams in their eyes, they went to each thug on the ground, and kept a boot on their back. We didn't need them jumping back up.

Jed noticed a new person on one knee, looking at him. Me!

"Mr. Cruz," Jed said, coming out of the stun of the sonic blast. "Impersonating a police officer is a felony."

"Why were you trying to buy Mr. Caret Senior's helmet from these guys?" I asked. "That seems to be an odd thing to do."

CHAPTER 52

Jed

Before we left the warehouse, I had to think things through. We had an army of thugs in our "custody." Letting them go back into the streets was easy to do, but was it the wisest? What I needed was for them all to disappear, so I called the real police on them—specifically, Organized Crime.

From there, we found a place to meet. There were so many in Metropolis, and I was not about to take the gangster to any of my favorite places.

"You stole it." Jed still couldn't believe it. "Who hired you to do that?"

"Master Jed, imagine my surprise when I learned from the police that a long time ago you were a gangster too, just like Caret."

"I'm no longer that person. I turned my life over to a higher power."

"But there you were, packing your gun, slicing and dicing bad guys with your own laser sword. Do they teach that in religious services now?"

"What do you want, Mr. Cruz? You stole the helmet to sell it?"

"I stole the helmet to see what Caret was up to. Then I learned one of Caret's former buddies wanted it."

"Logo," Jed said.

"Then you wanted it."

"Do you know what it is?"

"Well, yeah. Now that I know it's not the plans to build some kind of death moon to blow up a planet, I'm in more of a giving mood."

"Meaning what, Mr. Cruz?"

"I need answers. So, I'll sell it to you, and not Caret or Logo."

"Sell it to me? Isn't that illegal?"

"Or I could turn it over to the police."

Jed changed his tune fast. "No. Selling is good. Selling is the right thing to do. What answers do you need?"

"In my last case, I came across a criminal organization that was so powerful, and so evil, but no one knew it existed. Imagine a criminal mastermind so beyond every other, but not a gangster around knew this criminal existed. This criminal pitted one gangster against another, set up one gangster, and made them think it was another."

"Caret didn't try to whack me."

"I bet Caret has no idea what almost happened to you."

Jed gave a heavy sigh. "Okay, Mr. Cruz. You've got my attention."

"Watching the news lately?"

"Everyone in Metropolis is, Mr. Cruz. No actors will ever be wanting to do a ride-along with you."

"Was Caret involved?"

"In all this?" He laughed. "No. He only wanted to get control of a studio. It's not an act. He wants to make movies."

I showed him the picture of a man.

"Max. He's involved?"

"He goes by Beta Max these days. You know him?"

"I remember him."

"What's your scam?"

"My scam? I don't have a scam."

"One gangster in movies. One involved with politics. Another in virtual reality. And you, with a religious institution."

"Caret and Logo hate each other and have been trying to kill each other forever. I don't like Caret and would never work with him. Logo never has asked me to work with him. Max, or Beta Max, is a bum. No one will work with him."

"Sitting here, talking it out, I realize this criminal mastermind is much bolder."

"Your shadowy criminal mastermind that no one knows about? Why is he is so much bolder."

"Because you're part of it."

"I'm part of it?"

"Part of it, but don't know it—like Caret and Logo. I know Caret's scam, the Movie-Town scandal."

"Caret wasn't one of the ones arrested."

"No, he was the person to get my criminal overlord into that world."

"So, I'm the doorway for your criminal overlord into my religious world?"

"Jed, she tried to kill you once. I bought you some time, but she'll come back at you. This is clean-up time. She's going to erase all the clues she can, so I can't figure out what she's doing." I stood up from the table. "You are going to be a very dangerous person to be around."

"She? I thought your criminal overlord was a man."

"If you want to buy the helmet, it's best if we do business sooner rather than later. I'll figure out what you're up to as well, even if you're dead or disappeared."

"She?"

"How much are you going to pay me for the helmet?"

"I know who you're talking about—NeuroDancer."

"Why would you say the name of some dance celebrity?"

"Stop it, Cruz. You can stop the act. She's the common denominator."

"How is she the common denominator?"

"She's dating Caret and Logo. I was dating her, too. She's still, supposedly, married to Max."

"What kind of religious leader are you?" I asked.

"I know—bad. I'm a bad one. What did you expect from a gangster?"

Jed was suddenly a different person, sweating, looking around—scared. "You're right, Cruz. You are smart. It's her. I want protection. I'll tell you my end, but I need protection."

CHAPTER 53

The Mayor

I had asked Wilford G., Jr. to accompany me to City One for the meeting. The fact that I could call a senior meeting with the Mayor of Metropolis, the Police Chief of Metropolis, and senior City Hall staff, as a civilian, was nothing to brag about. I felt I had arrived full circle to where I had begun as a detective—they hated me.

Wilford G., Jr was for credibility. They liked him. When we first arrived, all the aides talked to him, but acted as if I weren't even there. I was the one who'd asked for the meeting but they acted as if I was the Invisible Man. The fallout from the Movie-Town scandal was still happening. The owner of one of the major newsfeed chains had been arrested, including the managing editor, and the editors of arts and entertainment. Good grief, it was never going to end.

We were in Mayor Likegate's massive office, seated at his desk. The Mayor wasn't there yet, but his senior aide, Mr. Frame, was sitting in a chair on the side of the mayor's desk, and on the other side was a man I'd never seen before. Finally, he seemed to read my mind, and said, "I'm with the Metro FBI office."

No wonder he didn't introduce himself. I think I got his predecessor fired.

Chief Hub came in with three men; two of them were the Organized Crime guys I had been working with. They all sat in chairs placed behind us. I didn't like that, because I didn't like people behind me that I couldn't see, but that's how it was.

The Mayor came in, and they all stood, except me. Since I needed to play nice at this meeting, I stood too.

"Gentlemen, have a seat."

He walked over to his desk, and sat—no handshakes from him this time.

"Mr. Cruz, it's your meeting," he said.

"Thank you, Mayor. The reason I wanted to meet, was to bring you into what I'm doing, because of the nature of what's going on. As a result of what I'm calling the Movie-Town Conspiracy Case, I felt I needed to be more delicate in how I move forward."

"You mean the collateral damage," the Mayor interjected.

"I don't know what you mean by that."

"The dead bodies we keep coming across. The ones you killed directly. I heard your wife joined in on the fun. The suicides. We had a situation today, where one of these studio people killed his entire family before killing himself."

"That's not my fault. Why should I get blamed for that? They were crooks; they tried to kill me, and they got caught."

The Mayor said nothing.

"I do have feelings. I remember when we were in police custody at SAG headquarters, and the head of the studio lied his way in, so that he could talk to me. He was a shattered man. He would have done anything, paid me anything, not to blow the case wide open. He was one of the first Movie-Town suicides. I should have done something. I could have gotten him to talk, reveal evidence. But, he could have also been one of the ones that sent two movie stars to kill me. I still don't know, and probably never will. All of this, could have been managed better, but it's not as if we have precedence for this. How do you prepare for something like this?" I looked around at everyone.

"I want to do the next part differently," I added.

"Next part," the Fed asked, "what next part?"

"This is not over."

"What does that mean?" I heard Chief Hub's voice behind me.

"This is the beginning of the case, not the end."

I couldn't stand people sitting behind me, that I could not see. I got up and walked to a movable white board about 10 feet from us. It was on wheels, so I pulled it closer to all of us. I drew one big circle, then a second one in the middle, and then a third.

"I believe this is the work of one master criminal. I am operating under the theory that everything this person is involved in, is part of this grand plan. We are here." I pointed to the first circle. "This part of the plan is smashed. The Movie-Town scheme was the financing."

"Financing?" Mr. Frame asked.

"To do whatever this person is going to do."

"I think I know what the third circle is, but I'm not positive. I don't know what the second circle is. That second part is what I need to know. I do have one clue. Prime Numbers."

Frame shot a look at the Mayor.

"Mr. Cruz, are you are accusing the most prestigious political consulting firm on the planet of criminality? A firm that has gotten me elected Mayor, your police friend there elected, city councilmen and councilwomen, Metropolis judges, senators, congresspeople. This firm has had a spotless record for more than a century."

"Has a client of theirs ever lost an election?" I asked.

A few of the men laughed.

"Cruz, you don't know anything," Frame said.

"I know. That's why I'm here. I know nothing about politics."

"Ninety-nine percent of the time, the person who raises the most money is going to win," Frame continued. "Prime Numbers picks winners in their clients. They don't take everyone who wants to hire them. You have to prove to them that you're a viable candidate, and a winner. For those races, where both sides have lots of money, Prime Numbers is the master in the industry of making sure you win."

"Do you have any proof whatsoever that there's criminality involved?" the Fed asked.

"Can an election be rigged?"

Now everyone was laughing, except Wilford G., Jr.

"No, Mr. Cruz," Mr. Frame answered. "It literally is the most scrutinized activity in the universe. Not that criminals and corporations haven't tried. Do you have anything more than that?"

"If I had told any of you that there was criminality involving the major movie studios of Metropolis, you would have said I was crazy too, and it was impossible. If I'd told you SAG accountants, and two of the biggest movie stars in the world tried to kill me, in my own vehicle, you all would have laughed me out of this room. But isn't that what happened? You're still arresting people. People are still swallowing bottles of sleeping pills, slitting wrists, and blowing their brains out."

They were all silent.

"This criminal is the cleverest criminal we've ever come across. The movie studios were for the money. I need to figure out the second part."

"You say you know what the third one might be. What's that?" one of the OC guys asked.

"Virtual reality—but forget that one. We need to figure out circle number two. It's Prime Numbers. I'm positive of it. I need a crash course in every aspect of what the company does. The scam, like the studios releasing ancient movies as new blockbusters, may be right in front of our eyes, but we don't know what we're seeing."

"Mr. Cruz, I know everyone at Prime Numbers. So does my staff," the Mayor said. "They are the most honest, hardworking people I have ever worked with in politics. Their reputations are beyond reproach. You're wrong on this."

"Do you have pictures of their staff? I couldn't find anything on the Net," I asked.

"Oh no, not the pictures again," Chief Hub said.

"No, Mr. Cruz, you wouldn't find any photos of the Prime Numbers staff on the Net or any database. They're classified, due to the sensitive nature of the work they do for government, and their anonymity is maintained precisely to keep our elections free from even the appearance of corruption—which you are now intimating has been corrupted."

The Mayor turned his attention to the Chief, and said, "Yes, we do know how Mr. Cruz excels at identifying criminals, when he has a photo gallery before him. Okay, Mr. Cruz, we'll play." The Mayor turned to Mr. Frame. "Get the photos from the last party we had. I think all of them were there."

Frame got up from his seat with a sigh, and disappeared out the side door.

"I hope I'm wrong," I said to the Mayor.

"I hope you're wrong too." He had a thought. "Do you realize what this would do, if you turned out to be right?"

"I just need to know what the scam is, so I can figure out this criminal's ultimate plan."

"You don't realize what it means," the Mayor continued. "It would nullify every election they've ever been involved with."

I was taken aback. "No, it wouldn't."

"Yes, it would."

"No. I was saying that to Wilford G., Jr."

"Mr. Cruz, that's a union. That's not an official elective office. However, losing sides would be able to contest the results in a court of law, which means the results could be set aside."

Mr. Frame returned with a tablet, with the first photo already on the screen.

"These are from the Prime Numbers' Christmas Party," the Mayor said. "It's funny that I saw you that same day, after I came from their party, the Council of Corporations Party. You caused a bunch of trouble there, too, if I remember."

I ignored him, and placed the tablet on the Mayor's desk. I looked at the faces.

"How about going to the photo with all of the staff in the same photo?" The Mayor swiped until we got to the photo.

I stared. "Who's that?"

"That's Wizard," Frame said. "He's their chief strategist and pollster."

"Who's that?"

The men were all gathered around, and they were all getting nervous.

"That's Mr. Euclid, he's the President of Prime Numbers."

"I was at the home of Mr. Cruces—the Man of the Galaxy. He hired me for a case. I wrapped it up. The two of them were waiting in the lobby of his house. I had a distinct feeling they came there, so they could see me in person."

"A feeling, Mr. Cruz." Frame laughed. "That's no kind of evidence."

"This man here," I pointed to a third man. "He's the guy from that diner. I was supposed to meet this new client for a case—a Mr. Jones. He sent another man to the office to leave the retainer."

"Mr. Jones?" the Chief said.

"Yes. It was the diner that had the hovercar bomb. The hovercar parked right near the entrance that I would have walked through. I was on the video-phone the whole time, and pretended it cut off after the explosion. That man couldn't run out of that diner fast enough."

The men were speechless, and all of them looked sick.

CHAPTER 54

The Visitor

They all believed me now.

The Organized Crime guys were now going to put together an entire task force. Frame disappeared from the room. Wilford G., Jr. spent his time on the mobile phone. Hub was also immediately on his mobile.

"Let's arrest him," Hub said.

"Not yet," I said. "We need to find more before we move. We have no evidence."

"Of course we have no evidence, but we can see if we can rattle him in interrogation," Hub said.

I looked at the Mayor. "We'll never get him in interrogation, unless we are officially going to charge him for attempted murder. We don't have any solid evidence for that. My say-so won't be enough. Any Free City first-year lawyer could beat the rap."

"Mr. Cruz is right. We have nothing. What are you going to do?" the Mayor asked.

"I'm going to do my private detecting, and bring the Chief some evidence," I answered.

"Mr. Cruz, we appreciate what you did here today, but I think the Chief should assign you some police protection."

"It's okay. I have bodyguards with me at all times. Besides, if we do that, then they'll really know I'm onto them."

"Based on your feelings," the Mayor added, "and a bomb, they already know you're onto them."

"But they know we have nothing. Let's use the appearance of a police cruiser strategically."

"The people at Prime Numbers are no dummies, Mr. Cruz. They're smarter than any politician-type out there, even me."

"I'm a civilian, Mr. Mayor."

It was a gamble, telling them about Prime Numbers, especially when virtually all of them were clients and friends with the firm. But I had worked with them long enough to know that even with that being the case, they had no use for criminals in Metropolis.

I flew out of Police One feeling some sense of accomplishment. I had identified Rogue Three. Mr. Hovercar Bomber was a Prime Numbers employee. So, it wasn't just accountants and actors trying to kill me. Political consultants had jumped in on the action, too. Well, I had no problem with kicking Mr. Hovercar Bomber out of a vehicle to his death, either.

My plan for the day was set, until I received a call in the Pony. I wasn't making *that* mistake again, until my arch-villain nemesis was no longer out there. In the passenger seat was Sidewalk Sally Jane. She was tall, buff, and brawny, the perfect female muscle for me at this time. In the back seat were two more sidewalk sallies, Teal and Indigo. They were my shooters.

Sidewalk Sally Jane answered the call. "Liquid Cool Detective Agency."

"Cruz!" It was PJ. "Get back to the office right away. You won't believe what's happening."

"What's happening?"

"She's here."

"Who's there?"

"Who do you think?"

We got to Liquid Cool as quickly as we could. By this time, it was all over the newsfeed. NeuroDancer was in Buzz Town for an impromptu pop-up performance. It was something performers did all the time. They'd just show up in some part of the supercity, to give a free show for the people. Pop-ups, as their name suggested, were set-up on the fly, at any kind of venue you could think of.

News hovertrucks were in the sky, and there were already crowds of fans on the streets below—right in front of my Liquid Cool building. We all waited in the offices, and watched the television. The best publicity was always free publicity, and she was getting a ton of it today. I watched the Dame do her dance number.

"Tell us immediately if you start feeling funny," PJ said to me.

I smiled a bit. "Don't worry, I will."

"You don't think she's going to come up here?" PJ asked.

"That is exactly what she's going to do. This is all a ruse for her to come see me."

The street performance went on for about 30 minutes. Pop-ups were never that long. The celebrity was in, out, and the pop-up was folded up for next time. That's how it was with this one. Her singing and dancing was over, and it was time for what would take up her time for hours:

signing autographs, taking pictures, mingling with fans, and walking around visiting places of business—all with a camera crew in tow.

I heard the beep of the elevator, and the quiet was replaced by an explosion of noise: talking, footsteps, laughing. She came around the corner. Immediately behind her were her male fellow dancers. Behind them were the camera crew, her business team, her P.R. team, her security team, and all the fans, a never-ending flow of fans.

I was standing outside my office, waiting. Behind me was my main three-woman sidewalk sally team. Behind them were seven more sidewalk sallies. Behind them was PJ, hiding her shotgun behind her back.

NeuroDancer walked up to me and stopped about a foot from me. Her outfit was just like a celebrity, meaning nice on the eyes, but completely impractical. The main feature was her mesh halter top open from under her visible bra to above her waist. She had abs of steel, with a pierced navel, and the piercing looked like some kind of expensive ruby. In a supercity that rained all the time, this was not the kind of thing to wear. But it was NeuroDancer. She could do whatever she wanted.

"Don't hate me 'cause I'm beautiful, Mr. Cruz," she said playfully with that upper-class, faux-British accent of hers.

I smiled.

She looked at the sidewalk sallies around me, and started laughing.

"Mr. Cruz, I never knew you had your own personal female body guard service."

"They make sure I don't do any rooftop dancing on ledges."

"Mr. Cruz, you have to live on the wild side every now and then."

"As long as that living doesn't lead you to dying."

She laughed again, and turned to everyone behind her. "This is Mr. Cruz of the famous Liquid Cool detective agency. If you ever need a private detective, he's your man. He never stops, never quits, no matter the cost. Sadly, all great protagonists have an Achilles heel, though. A fatal flaw that always leads to their personal destruction."

I held up a data disk from my pocket. "My wife has always told me I have to learn more about pop-culture. She gave me every single song you ever recorded. She even found those secret ones you did under another name, back when you were just a stripper-dancer-singer, before you became the NeuroDancer. My favorite song was: 'I Will Rule the Galaxy.'

"The fatal flaw of every arch-villainess is they can never keep their mouth shut."

At that moment, the Dame was not smiling. There was no facade. She was her true self before me. I could see the menace in her eyes.

"Do you think our fatal flaws will consume us at the same time?" she asked me.

"I don't believe your undoing will be all that epic. It will be very simple—very final."

"I was about to say the same about you."

"I look forward to that final chapter, then."

"You have a great day, Mr. Cruz." She turned to her entourage and fans. "Didn't I tell you all that Mr. Cruz is such a great actor!"

They all exploded in applause.

"My agent wants him to play my leading man in the movie. I say he's perfect for the role. Don't you agree?"

Her sycophants yelled every version of "yes" there was.

"Let's go everyone!" She led the way.

The NeuroDancer led her people back the way they came, back to the elevators. It would take a good 15 minutes before the last of them was gone.

We all went back into the office.

"Cruz," PJ said to me, as she put her shotgun back under her desk. "I never thought I would say this, since I'm a secretary, and not a gang member anymore, but that woman is too dangerous to leave walking around alive. Don't taunt her. She's going to kill you, you know."

"She's going to try—but we knew that before she came here to play her games. She came here, because she's scared of something. 'Scared' is good. 'Scared' means she'll make mistakes. Or, it could just be what she wants me to think, and I'm still the rat in her maze. So am I the man, or the rat?"

"Too much talk," PJ said. "Find a legal way to go shoot her, before she makes you shoot yourself dead."

CHAPTER 55

Mrs. Meta

Every word the Dame had said to me, I played over and over in my head. I assumed that every sentence had a double meaning, that every word could be a clue. Coming to Liquid Cool was either an act of panic, or part of her grand plot. I had to proceed believing both possibilities were true, until I knew which it was.

Also, I'd never believed in coincidences. Why now? I had removed one of her players from the board. I had whisked Jed away into hiding, a task I was becoming very good at, and learned another piece of the puzzle as to what her grand scheme was.

Had Mr. Meta lived, I would have spoken to him, even from his jail cell. I knew why the Dame was involved with the Movie-Town scandal. My assumption was solid. It was the bank account for her ultimate plot, but I was going to talk to everyone anyway. If I were going to defeat my arch-nemesis, I couldn't be cocky. Wilford G. had said it in his book, *How to be a Great Detective with 100 Rules*: Never cut corners or skip steps. Private detective work is about following all the steps, following procedure, not to bore you, but to eliminate assumptions that might be right or might be wrong. It's the steady-Eddie, non-glamorous, shoe-to-pavement, finger-to-keyboard investigating work that solves cases, not pretending to be some modern version of Sherlock Holmes. A guess is a guess; evidence is not a guess.

When I arrived at the estate of Mr. Meta in Opus Fields, I felt one of two possible things was going to happen. Mrs. Meta and family were either going to talk to me because they couldn't believe I had the nerve to show my face, or they would see who could shoot me first. I felt it was a risk worth taking.

They even had their own valets in the parking lot of the tower.

"Can I ask you a personal question?" I asked the valet.

From his cold demeanor, I could tell he knew exactly who I was.

"Should I dial 9-1-1 now?"

He smirked. "Does your sense of humor impress the ladies?"

"I'm married, so I only have one lady to impress. She's always impressed."

"I'm not. Don't concern yourself, sir. I'll dial the meat wagon, if it comes to that. Police won't be needed here."

"Good to know."

A butler met me on the elevator capsule, and he was not happy to see me either.

He pressed the stop button on the elevator.

"Why are you here?" he asked. His eyes were red with anger.

"I'm not here to cause any pain," I said.

He pushed the "go" button, and we were rising to the top again.

When we reached the 400th floor, still another 10 floors to the penthouse section, I saw the boxes. I followed the butler, and as we walked through the living room area, everything was boxed up, or wrapped up, about to be boxed up.

He took me to a smaller sitting room, which meant it was still bigger than my place.

I sat, and the butler was gone.

I had left my sidewalk sally bodyguards in the Pony, but had my special panic-button wrist band in case the Dame jumped out from behind a chair to make me go zombie. I also kept a hand on my piece in the shoulder holster. What I was doing was extremely dangerous. A grieving wife. The catalyst for her husband's suicide sitting in his place.

The door opened, and Meta's wife came in. She stood there, with her hands on her waist, and watched me.

"You are either the dumbest man I ever met or the bravest," she said.

I stood, and took a very humble tone. "I'm not here to cause any pain to the family—"

"No need to repeat your speech, Mr. Cruz. I heard you say it in the elevator with my butler. Sit back down." I did and she sat in the adjacent chair. "Normally, I offer refreshments, but it would be inappropriate to offer the murderer of my husband refreshments."

"Mrs. Meta, I didn't murder your husband. He killed himself. I killed Tuck Rogers. That I did. My wife killed Perfect Tony. She did that. However, I didn't kill your husband."

"You're as bad as someone in a B-movie, killing people all over the place. Is that the life of a typical private detective?"

"We're in Metropolis."

"Yes, that's true. Everything is bigger and badder here in Metropolis. The movies were bigger too, until you came along. Did the entire staff of the Screen Actors Guild really try to kill you right in the hallway of their offices?"

"They did."

"How do you cope with all this, all these people trying to kill you?"

"Yeah, I may need therapy soon."

"Save your money. Most therapists need therapists. Most therapists need to be in Metro Insane Asylum. Take it from a woman who's spent plenty on them—for herself, and her children.

"Enough of the small talk. What possessed you to come here, Mr. Cruz? As you can see from the packing, I won't be here long. My lawyers said I have to prepare to live a more modest lifestyle. My husband's estate is going to be sued into bankruptcy and worse. The children and I will be lucky to hold onto one home, let alone all seven of them."

"If your husband had lived, I would have asked for his advice for my current case."

"How ironic, isn't it? He hired the man who would lead to his own death."

"Was your husband involved in getting Tuck Rogers and Perfect Tony to kill me?"

She glared at me for a moment. "You are a cold, heartless bastard. No. My husband was greedy. He was a serial adulterer. He wasn't a murderer, and didn't get anyone to do murders for him. You already know who did—SAG. It's definitely something they would do. Immoral. Amoral. The media is saying organized crime took over the studios, but that's a lie. Gangsters didn't need to take over the studios to do bad things. They're already bad people. I know. I'm one of them."

"Do you know a man named Caret?" I showed her a picture.

"No."

"Any of these men?"

"No." I showed her another picture. "Why, everyone knows her, Mr. Cruz."

"Was she involved in the movie business too?"

"She was about to get into the biz in a big way. When you reach her level of fame and fortune, they all want to be in the movies. My husband's company tried to bid for one of her projects, but lost out to others. What is this about, Mr. Cruz?"

"If I wanted to get a list of every current and planned movie project of the NeuroDancer, and everyone who was involved, could you help me?"

"Why would I do that? Why would I help you do anything?"

"You've told me your life, and your children's, is in ruin, that your fortune will be gone after all the lawsuits are done."

"The word you're looking for is 'broke,' Mr. Cruz."

"You'll need money."

"You're going to lend me some money, Mr. Cruz? You're going to pay me to help you?"

"Even better: I'll give you the exclusive rights to a story of one of the greatest villains in Metropolis. A former stripper, currently world-famous dance performer involved with, and controlling four different gangsters, in a plot, quite literally, to take over the galaxy. The tip of the plot was the Movie-Town scandal, which a lone detective inadvertently exposed. SAG people tried to kill the detective to defend their illegal empire. The villain tried to kill the detective, because she desperately wanted to prevent him from finding out the illegal empire was going to finance the next phases of her grand scheme."

"Mr. Cruz, is any of this babbling true?"

"You couldn't make up something so incredible."

"If she's such a great villain, why are you still alive?"

"Will you help me?"

"Of course not. No one would believe such a story. No network would buy such nonsense. The Movie-Town scandal is a mini-series I'm already working on. I don't need you for that. Four gangsters? Is that the pictures of the men you showed me? You're making it all up, because you think you can con a grieving wife.

"I'm actually not grieving. Mr. Meta and I have been separated for years. The children hated him. We simply lived in the same apartment, but it's so big we'd never see him. You can't con me, Mr. Cruz. I've seen the best con artists out there in the movie biz. Even the worst of them is better than you." I sat back in my chair, smiling.

"Why are you smiling? I'm not going to help you, and I'm about to call my butler and have you thrown out and barred from this building."

"When I was being held by the police in the SAG headquarters building, your husband pretended to be my lawyer, so he could be let in to talk to me. He wanted to bribe me not to disclose what I knew to the world. He knew the life he knew was about to end. He didn't care about the money. He would have given it all to me right there, if he could have kept his reputation as a great movie maker, not a fraud who peddled ancient movies to the public as his own. You should have seen his eyes. He was a broken and desperate, pitiful person in front of me, not the larger-than-life movie mogul I had known.

"I heard he committed suicide, and I was disturbed. I still am. I wish I could have made a deal with him. I didn't owe him anything, but I didn't think all this was fair to his family. I knew all of this was just a small part of a grand plot of a shadowy criminal. All these people died, and were going to die, because of her, not me. I was going to be the one who stopped her."

"Do you have a screenplay?" she asked.

"I'm still solving the case. I'm a detective, not a screenplay writer."

"'Screenwriter,'" she corrected. "I want exclusive rights. That means no one else. I can't form the company now, or it will get attached to all the lawsuits, but when the lawyers say I can, I get exclusive rights, first look, 10-year option, veto power on all above-the-line talent."

"I want a producer credit."

She smiled at me. "So, you're not the dumbest man I ever met."

CHAPTER 56

All the Kings Men

I could never forget this was a race. The Dame knew I was after her. Chief Hub once called me the luckiest man in the world. I was. She was more interested in "controlling the galaxy," than in killing me. It was the same for me. I was more interested in stopping her plot, than dealing with her. The rooftop incident was proof that she was human. I had moved her to anger, but she wasn't going to fall prey to her own emotions again. Feline, not canine. Cunning, not killing. Again, was I my own man, or her rat in a maze?

Phishy had finished the second task I'd assigned him. I had all the results compiled and collated. Phishy had every male sidewalk johnny working at the task, and they, in turn, had all their trustworthy friends working at the tasks. Metropolis was a city of 50 million people. Fortunately for the task, most didn't vote.

The day had arrived.

I was not in my trademark tan fedora and slicker. Today, I was in a standard black suit with white shirt. No hat. Just a plain Average Joe in a suit. My wife almost didn't recognize me out of "uniform."

I drove to Police One in the Pony, and a spot had been reserved for me in the special guest parking level. Two police officers were assigned to watch my vehicle. I was led by another officer to another level. Chief Hub was also in a standard suit and tie. Like most law enforcement, even when not in uniform, and in civilian attire, they looked as if they were in uniform. With Hub was the new local Fed Chief and the Chief of the Metropolis Marshal Service—Hub told me they had to accompany us too.

We waited for Mr. Massimo to arrive. The well-dressed tall man did, 20 minutes later. Hub introduced me to him.

We drove to Prime Numbers in three hovercars. One of the vehicles had my three sidewalk sally bodyguards (well, that's what I told everyone they were for), who were dressed in female business attire, courtesy loan from Metro PD. No fedoras for them, either.

Prime Numbers was in Silicon Dunes, and it was a monolith tower on a hill all by itself. It radiated power and prestige. We flew into their secure parking lot, and were met by valet staff who promptly took the hovercars to park, as others led us to the elevator banks.

Before we entered the main offices, we were all scanned by non-humanoid robots. A female aide greeted all of us, and took us to a waiting room where we were served refreshments. When we were almost done with drinks, the female aide returned to the room, and escorted us out.

We were led along the open area of the firm, with seemingly hundreds of cubicles with employees hard at work. I noticed him. Mr. Hovercar Bomber was one of the workers standing up, drinking from a metal cup. He almost choked on whatever he was drinking. I ignored him. He wasn't going anywhere.

Mr. Euclid was the founder and president of Prime Numbers. He knew every politician on the planet, and elected leaders Up-Top too. His firm wasn't an official member of the Council of Corporation; they couldn't be, due to conflicts of interest, but they were as much leaders in the corporate world as they were in the government world. After all, if you were a CEO or megacorp senior VP, who were you going to call, if you wanted to be a powerful elected official for a couple of terms or more?

Mr. Euclid was the first man I'd seen watching me when I was at Mr. Cruces's residence to wrap up the case. The second man was now standing next to him.

"Mr. Massimo," Mr. Euclid said, graciously greeting him. "It's good to see you again."

"These are all my people. I hope you don't mind."

"Not at all, Mr. Massimo. For the journey you're about to embark on, you'll need far more people than this."

The office was magnificent. It seemed as if everything were carved out of diamonds. There were exactly the right number of chairs already assembled. He directed us to take our seats. Massimo sat in the middle; with my sidewalk sallies and me on one side; Hub, the Fed, and the Marshal on the other.

"Mr. Massimo, you remember my genius partner. We call him Wizard. He's our wizard when it comes to winning elections."

The two men shook hands, and now we were all ready to sit and start the meeting.

"Thanks for meeting me on such short notice," Massimo said.

"Not at all," Mr. Euclid said. "It shows passion on your part."

"I've talked to everyone you said I should. The spouse, kids, family, close friends and colleagues. I'm going to do it. Despite all the skeletons in my closet, I'm going to do it."

"Excellent," Mr. Euclid said. "There is no skeleton in a closet that can't be mitigated in politics. That's not the issue. The issue is you not minding that everyone knows about those skeletons in your closet."

"Yes, so true. I don't mind, and the people I care about don't either."

"Excellent."

"Are your finances in order?" Mr. Euclid asked.

"Yes. I'll be able to transfer my first payment today if we can map out our next 24 months before the election. Is it enough time?"

"Excellent. Yes. It is a short window, but we'll have no problem building a successful team and launching a winning campaign."

"You have some new members on your team." Wizard spoke finally, and he was looking at no one else but me.

"Yes, I do," Mr. Massimo said.

"Mr. Massimo," Mr. Euclid began, "is there some reason why you've brought a private detective person to our offices, along with the Chief of Police, new head of the Metro FBI office, and head of the Metro Marshal's Service? Are they to be your senior advisers for a unique law and order policy platform you want us to create?"

Now it was my turn.

"I know," I said.

The two Prime Numbers men were quiet for a while.

"Know?" Mr. Euclid asked. "Know what?"

"I know," I repeated.

"I don't know what you're talking about."

"I'm going to give you and your friend a chance. I didn't do that with the movie studio people. They begged me to give them a chance, but it was too late. They didn't try to blow me up with a hovercar bomb, but they tried to kill me just the same. I was so mad that I didn't want to hear them, even though there was vital information I could have gotten from them.

"This time, I'm calmer, no anger. I'm here in a nice suit, sitting calmly, just talking. I'm offering what I didn't offer them, that chance. Cooperate, give us the information I need, and we'll be lenient."

"I don't know what you think is going to happen here—"

I interrupted Mr. Euclid before he could finish. "I'm not talking about your employee you told to set me up and try to blow me up with the hovercar bomb. I'm sure you did everything perfectly, so as not to connect either of you with him. There are no traces we could find to tie any of you to the guy who paid the money to get me to the diner, to the money, or the bomb, any of it. But I'm not talking about that. No one cares about that. I care about why. That's what I want to know.

"For the Movie-Town scandal the answer was always in front of us. The movies themselves. Ancient movies passed off as 'new' movies— pocket not just the multi-billion dollar profits, but also multi-hundred-million dollar production budgets. The answer was always right in front of our eyes—we just didn't know it.

"So, what does Prime Numbers do? You win elections. How do you win an election? A single vote. Whoever has the most, wins. Prime Numbers always wins. It always makes sure you, the client, get more votes than the other guy. But, you can't rig an election. Everyone told me so. Too bad I never listen to what everyone tells me, especially when I know they're wrong.

"It was very basic, actually. I had my people go out there with all that voter information. I figured we needed to go back five years at least, but it might be two elections, so we went back a decade. I interned for the head of the CIC at Metro Central, and she drilled that into me: you have to look for the pattern, you have to look for the pattern.

"I sent my people to interview each person that voted. We had all the elections they'd voted in. That's public information, but who they voted for is private and confidential. My people went out and interviewed everyone who was listed as voting for a given election. I picked key elections, elections where both rival candidates had lots of money. One was your client, the other wasn't.

"We found our first one. The man said he hadn't voted in 30 years, but the voting records said he had voted in every election in the last 30 years. Then we found our 30th, and then our 500th. We kept going. I wanted a big number for us to research.

"Once we had the data, then we went to the video tapes. Do you know in the past they verified votes by signature? Of course you know. You're a political firm. I have to confess, I don't vote, which is a bad thing, and I will stop that bad behavior immediately, but the way we verify the vote now is by fingerprints. All you need really is a thumb.

"Now, there are a lot of people with bionic hands or arms. For cyborgs who vote, they have a special serial number ID. That's how we do it for them. It was funny, when we reviewed the polling place recordings of all these people who were listed as voting but swore they never did. We saw a funny thing. Using all kinds of fancy technology, we saw cyborgs with fingerprints. The poll workers didn't notice it, but the cameras did. But cameras don't talk; they don't notice things like that, but we did.

"Cyborgs don't have fingerprints. They're not supposed to. And if they did, why unique fingerprints of people who'd never voted, but the system showed they had? Once we found out how you did it, it all came together from there. It was the same people, often coming back in disguises over and over and over again. It was the same districts. We were even able to tie all of them back here to you. You were careful never to pay them with Prime Numbers money, but someone had to pay them. Once we knew the people we were looking for, we were able to find out who was paying them. Once we had that, we were able to pick them up, and eventually, tie them back to you two."

While I was talking, I watched the two men slowly fall apart in front of our eyes. They tried to remain stoic, but even if it weren't perceptible to themselves, the men were red, sweating and trembling. They had that same look Mr. Meta had, the last time I saw him.

I pulled the photo from my jacket, opened it, and showed them.

"I want you to tell me how any one of these three people are involved in your scam."

The two men stared at the photos. Wizard seemed to drift off.

Mr. Euclid didn't look at the photos long. He was emotionally crumbling. He jumped from his chair and let out a yell. Suddenly, he was running for his desk. Hub, the Fed, and the Marshal were on top of him before he could shoot himself with the gun he'd pulled from the desk drawer. They pinned him to the ground as Mr. Euclid started crying like a lunatic. It was over.

Wizard stood up. "We don't know any of those people," he said, crying. "We don't know any of them. We never saw those people. We know the woman, everybody does, but never met her. Help me. I can't go to jail."

The Marshal returned to place handcuffs on him, too.

"I'll be back," I said to them. They gave me questioning looks.

I ran out of that room so fast, my sidewalk sallies could barely keep up. The hovercar bomber probably was watching the closed door all that time, and darted out of his cubicle. I chased him down, with an office full of workers standing and staring, tackled him, then proceeded, figuratively, to kick the living stuffings out of him.

CHAPTER 57

The Election Lady

The hovercar bomber was handcuffed to his hovergurney and carried out of the offices with three police officers accompanying the two ambulance medics.

Mr. Euclid had to be put into a straightjacket and carried out on another hovergurney. Wizard, at least, walked with his police escort to a police cruiser outside. Prime Numbers was now swarming with police, and all employees were barred from leaving the premises. They were all going to be here in the monolith tower, and interrogated well into the late of night. CSI came in and took every computer, file, device, and slip of paper.

We were in the lobby outside the gigantic glass doors to the main area, with the elevator back at the other end, waiting.

The group we were waiting for arrived. Before they came, Hub made a call, and soon after that call, the Mayor arrived, looking shattered. He and an aide, were waiting with Hub, the Fed, the Marshal chief, and me, when the group arrived. They were from Metro's Election Division—they were the agency that ran the elections process for the supercity.

Probably the only thing that kept them from being swept up in the coming scandal was that someone needed to be left standing to prosecute the criminals and restore the integrity of the process.

The woman who led the group to me also looked as if she had come out of a boxing match and lost.

She turned her attention to the Mayor. "Mr. Mayor, until this matter is resolved, you will have to relinquish your office. Has an interim person already been appointed?"

"Yes," he answered. "The police chief will be acting mayor of Metropolis."

"Fine. He will need to be sworn in today."

She turned her attention to me. A false smile on her face. "How on earth did you uncover this? The Chief called me. The local FBI called me. I told them it was impossible. Many have tried to subvert the voting process in this city, and they never could. We still looked. I put a team together to look anyway, myself. The Feds did. Organized Crime did. None could come up with how."

"Because you came at the problem from the standpoint that it was impossible to do," I said. "I came at the problem from the standpoint that it had already had been done, and was being done. Of course it was possible. Some criminal made it possible, and I wasn't going to be outdone by any criminal, no matter how smart they thought they were."

"Mr. Cruz, that is one thing none of us will ever say about you. No criminal is smarter than you." She looked up at the Mayor. "Mr. Mayor, please come with us."

I saw her people take out handcuffs.

"Wait," I said. "If it weren't for the Mayor, I couldn't have figured this out. I don't believe most of Prime Numbers' clients had any idea what was going on."

"Mr. Cruz, this scandal will negate every election in Metropolis for the last 10 years. Thank goodness you didn't decide to go back further, but it will probably come to that. Prime Numbers has been in business for 200 years."

"I don't believe it goes that far back, and now that you know what to look for, you'll find out for sure. Give the Mayor the benefit of the doubt. All of them should be given the benefit of the doubt. You'll find out soon who knew what and when. Criminals always leave a trail."

The election lady hesitated, and gestured for her agents to put away their handcuffs. "Mr. Cruz, we have to follow the election laws, and when it comes to real evidence of corruption in the voting process, the elected official is guilty until proven innocent. There will be multiple independent investigations and each election win will have to re-certified. However, no need to arrest anyone, yet.

"Mr. Cruz, is there more? The movie industry. Our entire political system. I want to know if there's more to come, so that I know if I need to increase my blood pressure medication."

"I'll answer that question at another time."

She thought for a moment. "I trust you can keep all of this confidential. Metropolis, in effect, has no political leadership whatsoever."

"It's not the end of the galaxy yet. Division heads can run everything in the interim. I'm a citizen. I'm not worried. Just keep the criminals from finding out. I'm sure you've heard I can keep a secret."

"Yes, I did hear that. I won't say any more." She turned to the Mayor. "Mr. Mayor."

The Mayor walked away with her and her people to the elevator banks. They entered when the capsule arrived, and were gone.

The three men looked at me. I glanced at my three sidewalk sally bodyguards, who were quietly watching me too.

Hub said, "In that meeting you said there were three circles."

"Four circles."

"Four circles?" the Fed said.

"Three are smashed, and there's the one left."

"Cruz," the Fed yelled out, flustered. "What fourth circle?"

"The Gangsters' Graveyard."

The men looked at me, incredulous looks on their faces.

"That doesn't exist."

"It does," I said.

"Where is it?" Hub asked.

"We can't shut it down, yet. In fact, you shouldn't be anywhere near it. We have to smash the third circle first."

"Cruz, there's no criminal mastermind who could conceive all this."

"You're right. She didn't. Others did. She was the one who knew what they were doing separately, and decided to take it all from them. Four gangsters. One girlfriend. Do I need to say any more?"

"What kind of detective are you?" the Fed asked. "I know of no private detective, no private investigation firm that has caused, or has been the center of so much trouble as you, in all my 40 years in law enforcement. I've only just met you, and I want to retire."

It was Master Jed's contribution to the NeuroDancer plot—the Gangsters' Graveyard. A place rumored in the crime world to be where one buried people never to be found again by the police. It was supposed to be an urban myth among the criminal class, but it was real.

Jed's story of working for Metro Trash Services and turning the mountains of trash the city produced every minute into great recycling, fuel, and building material was trash-talk. Maybe, Jed had stumbled upon the Graveyard by accident. Maybe, he was the one who had created it in the first place, deciding to make the myth into reality.

I wasn't allowed to get close to the site in Nil Point, but Metro police had the landfill site completely blocked off as 'White Shoes' arrived. They were the special CSI unit for high-profile external crime scenes. They didn't wear those white booties, but high-tech white hovershoes. They "walked" six inches above the ground on air, so not a strand of hair, a speck of dirt, or anything was disturbed, until it could be processed.

They never told me the full extent of what they found. I asked Hub how many bodies were buried there. He only answered, "A lot."

"How many is a lot?"

"A lot."

I didn't press further. I decided it was probably best if I didn't know after all.

PART SEVEN

Virtual Games

CHAPTER 58

NeuroDancer

No one in Metropolis would ever know the largest city on the planet had been, because of my private investigation, stripped of its political leadership. Even I would never know the full scope, since I didn't know politics, and had no desire to ever increase my knowledge in that area. What I did care about was the fact that a criminal had snared into her claws the ability to manipulate the very power of the supercity for her purposes. If I hadn't uncovered it, she would have been able to do whatever crimes she was planning, with the political leaders of Metropolis as her puppets.

I cut off her money. I cut off her power pawns-to-be. I cut off her means to dispose of the bodies of power-pawns-not-to-be—she was as diabolical as any psychopath out there. Now we came to the final piece—the means of control. I'd always suspected it was Beta Max and his virtual reality empire where her plot had originally sprung. But before I could tackle that final piece, I had to answer a question for myself. Was knowing you were a mind-control puppet of the Dame enough to resist, or eliminate, that power?

The Olympus Emporium was one of the largest venues in Metropolis. It was the site of every popular sporting game in the supercity. The set-up today was a huge crescent moon stage, opened out over a sea of round tables. You couldn't charge top price for dinner and drinks at a turbo-football or laser soccer game, but for the largest star in the world, the NeuroDancer would fill the stadium, and make all involved a tsunami of cash.

Looking around the venue from my table, it seemed everyone in the city was here. I scanned the crowd, and there were all walks of life here, from the Silicon Dunes gazillionaire types, to mid-city working class to Free City freeloaders. All these different people loved her music? I did notice that most of them were men, which wasn't surprising—a female dancer-singer with an all-female dance troupe—but based on my unique perspective about her, was quite disturbing.

At my table, flanking me, were my sidewalk sally bodyguards. Their job here was simple: watch me like a hawk. This was an experiment, and I was in the sole minority. PJ called me a "stupid man," Dot forbade me to go, and I had to spend over an hour getting her not to be worried. All the sidewalk sallies were adamantly opposed to what I was doing. But I had to know. Was I still her zombie or not? This was not a matter of male ego; it was a matter of life or death—my life.

How did I even get a ticket to the NeuroDancer Show? Scalpers, of course. I'd had Phishy pick them up days ago.

There was one. I saw Caret sitting at a table right next to the stage. I would never have had the money to buy those tickets. Caret was his flamboyant crazy self. I could hear him all the way from here, dozens and dozens of rows back. My eyes glanced over to the other side, and I noticed Logo sitting at his table with his gang.

Where's little piggy number three?

I looked all over, and then turned around. I looked at the tables behind me. Then my eyes looked up at the balconies. There was Beta Max. It was one of those ultraviolet sections, so in the dim light, his smile, tie, and hair looked like glowing phosphorous. Everyone in the section looked strange, with different parts of their body features and clothes glowing.

I hated these kinds of shows. The music band flew over the audience on a hoverplatform; the percussion was so loud that our glasses were rattling on our tables and in our hands. Dancers wearing jetpacks flew in, doing all their acrobatic tricks in the air. More members of the warm-up team flew by, to hover above the stage. There were fireworks, flashing lights, strobe lights, hoverlights. There were so many scantily-clad performers hovering around, not just above the stage now, but all over, flying around us. I felt it was a safety hazard. I didn't want sweat droplets falling into my drink, but then, I was a germophobe, and that's how our minds thought. I looked at my glass, and decided it was already contaminated, so I was done.

The noise, the lights. Then some guy ran out from behind the crowd, whipping up the crowd in a frenzy, by asking, "Is everyone ready for the show!" I said to myself, "No, we're not ready for the show. We just like to sit here in the dark, being bombarded with all this noise and blinding light, with naked people dripping sweat on us, our food, and drinks!" I was clearly not having fun.

I glanced at Sidewalk Sally Jane, and she shook her head at me, smiling.

"I never come to shows like this. I hate 'em," I said.

"I would never have guessed," she said back to me.

My other sidewalk sally was laughing at me too.

It all stopped. It was pitch black in the stadium. Not a sound. All the lights were off. It startled all of us, even me.

A single light appeared on the center of the stage. All the lights turned on, but all the hoverlights, the band, and hovering naked people were gone. There she was in her practically see-through outfit—the NeuroDancer.

Now, I had to put up with endless applause as most of the crowds took to their feet, yelling, catcalling, whistling. Her female dance troupe appeared behind her in plastic see-through outfits, rainbow-colored undergarments, hair, and make-up.

It was a perfectly choreographed performance of dancing, strutting, jumping, diving, flipping, gyrating. Those ladies worked that stage, because they performed on every inch of it. I did have to admire them, because what they were doing wasn't the dancer's version of running five miles; it was running three full marathons. They were in stellar shape, in peak performance. I'd expected a lot of hype, but, no, they could dance. No question about that. They would run circles around Dot and me, even at our best, and anyone else, at the Booty Shaker Dance Club.

The hour-long group performance, which involved an ever-changing holo-background and stage, brought every corner of the planet throughout time to us. The Neuro-dancers danced with cavemen, Roman Centurions, American Indians, Vikings, knights in armor, Japanese samurai, African warriors, soldiers from every world war every fought, then they switched to space, with gasps from the audience. They were dancing in space, on the stars, around black holes, in asteroid belts, with comets streaming by, planets orbiting.

Okay, even I was admitting it was a damn good show at this point.

Then it all stopped again. The strobe light was back for the end of the performance, the solo performance of the NeuroDancer. The effect was fog and smoke. It enveloped her, and the last number was a sultry, provocative one with her jumping from the stage, into the audience, to move between tables.

I watched Caret, who looked like a drooling child. She came within an inch of his face, pretending to kiss him. She moved throughout all the tables nearest the stage. Then she made it to Logo's table. He, too, looked like a hyper-hormonal teenager, staring at her as she did her pretend kiss.

As I watched, I knew my question was answered. In my mind's eye, I was composed and in control, except for one thing. That's exactly what I'd thought before PJ and Dot showed me the videotape recording of me at the NeuroDancer fashion show, where I'd looked just like Caret and Logo did. I was still under her influence, even now, and there was nothing I could do about it.

I tried to grit my teeth, or clench my fist. It was hopeless. I stared at her, and noticed she was staring directly at me. She was making her way to my table. The NeuroDancer danced on the table in front of mine, and did a dance routine just for me, then jumped down.

"Cruz," I heard her whisper her in my ear, and I could smell her perfume.

She moved away, back to the stage. There she took a bow to thunderous applause; everyone took to their feet. Then, she disappeared in a puff of smoke—even louder applause.

I felt myself being shook. After a few moments, I turned to look at my sidewalk sally bodyguards. They were standing, and were so far from having expressions of happiness, I thought they were going to drag me out of there at that very moment.

A young kid appeared, and invited me backstage. "She wants to see you," he said. My bodyguards forbade me. I ignored them, and went to the backstage VIP lounge. Except it wasn't a lounge; it was a slightly smaller version of the front area. Instead of tables, everyone was standing, packed in like sardines. They would stay in this cramped space for hours, days even, if only for the chance of seeing the NeuroDancer up-close.

I wasn't that desperate. I went straight for the bar, and planted myself on a stool at the farthest end. My two bodyguards stuck to me like glue, and I ordered a drink from the bartender.

Other than me, with my two sidewalk sallies, no one saw her. The NeuroDancer came out from a side door behind the bar, as the bartender was about to set my drink in front of me. All dancers and models were quick-change artists—she was now in a sleek black outfit. She took the drink from him, set it in front of me, and plopped a cherry right in the center.

"Mr. Cruz."

"Nova," I said.

"You remembered my first name. How touching. How's the private detective business?"

There obviously was a stool behind the bar. She sat on it, to lean on the bar, as she looked directly at me. I had her full attention.

"It's quite good, these days."

"What's with the fedora sisters behind you?" she asked. "Do they follow you everywhere?"

"Only those places where I might run into you."

She laughed.

"Am I that dangerous? I'm harmless." She batted her long eyelashes.

"I gotta wife, remember."

"Mr. Cruz, a little flirting never hurt anyone. You are what we refer to in the female world as a 'keeper.' You're not like one of those man-hoes you run into all the time in our circles. Why couldn't I be lucky, like your wife? I never could get the steak, always the soggy, sat-on hot dog. Never the silverware, always the cheap plastic utensils. Where's my Up-Top man? He doesn't even have to be from Up-Top. All he needs is that vibe."

"I was told you do all right."

"I'm a world-famous star. Plenty of boyfriends—no shortage of those, easy to come by. I need a real partner in crime."

"Bonnie and Clyde," I said.

"Yes, Mr. Cruz," she said, smiling. "The husband and wife gangsters of old, shot down in a hail of bullets. That's the way to go. It's too bad, Mr. Cruz. You could have been my Clyde."

"Yeah, but I don't like to get shot. Been there, done that. Not fun."

She laughed again.

"You've got me all wrong, Mr. Cruz. I'm just a dancer, in this mean, cold world, looking for my Clyde. It's too bad we didn't meet earlier in life. Things could have gone in a completely different way."

"I could have made an honest woman out of you."

"Or I could have made a dishonest man out of you. Maybe in the next life, Mr. Cruz."

"The next life, then." I raised my drink to her.

The NeuroDancer got up from her stool and disappeared back out the side door, unseen by all her fans, but seen in living color by me and my two sidewalk sallies.

CHAPTER 59

Tag

In my last big case, a client gave me a bonus. Such a thing was not unusual. I had many clients who paid me a bit extra for a job well done. However, this client gave me more money than the fees for the case—a lot more—so much more, that I didn't even put it in the bank.

I'd always wanted to have a secret stash of cash. It was like something out of a B-movie, where a couple had their secret stash, to use for their big getaway to a new life. For me, I'd found out why that client had given me all that money—he was getting rid of all his worldly possessions, and though he tried to kill me (yes, my client), I still missed him, and especially his sister, Sarah. *Now* I had found a use for all that money.

Phishy had found him for me. I was still feeling as if I were being followed, so I was relying on my associate much more than usual for legwork. Tag was a kid, just like Bite-Size, but Tag's special knowledge was the VR world. When not jacked-in, he did endless scraper jobs. There was so much garbage on the Net, lots of people paid data scrapers to sift through all of it, and give them a regular feed of what they wanted. And the wealthy never directly connected to the Net themselves—always through filter services or scrapers.

Beta Max had told me gangsters wanted to get the rights to his VR creation, The Five Rings of Babel. Did I believe him? Not for a second. I felt it was his ploy to throw me off track. He didn't know I knew all about his past affiliations with Caret and Logo—and Master Jed. Regardless, I needed to know the story behind the VR world, and, specifically, Beta Max.

"It's a decent VL, but not the best, and not the most popular—not even close."

Tag was a thin, sandy blond kid, who wore eyeliner, and whose hands up to his elbows were covered in tattoos. I never did get the eyeliner, and the black-painted fingernails, however, he was once a cybergoth. We sat in his bedroom, of all places, which he called his Command Base. He had a bed, more like a cot, and the room was filled with his VR consoles.

"Do you leave this room?" I asked.

I was sitting on the floor with him, because there were no chairs, only the lounge couches for the VR consoles.

"Yeah, all the time, Mr. Cruz. Why would you say that? It doesn't stink in here, does it? My clothes are fresh and fluffy clean."

I looked around more. "VL?"

"Virtual life. Or you can say the cyber cosmos, v.universe, or The V, or v-space—"

"Why all the new terms? Virtual reality, that's it, or even VR."

"They'll think you're a cyber-cop."

"What's wrong with that? They catch pervs and white collar crooks."

"Also cyberpunks."

"Only the ones trying to hack into the government."

"Seriously, don't say 'virtual reality' on the street. No one will trust you. How can you not know that? You were a hovercar guy."

"Yes, I was, but we weren't playing any VL games. We were racing, in real life. Tag, what do you have for me? Phishy said you know stuff. What about Beta Max?"

"I do know stuff. Everyone in the VL scene knows him. He's the President of VRA. The Virtual Reality Association."

"Which does what?"

"He oversees the quality of all new synths."

"Am I going to need a universal translator with you?"

He giggled. "You know nothing."

"I know nothing."

"The synth. It's the core data disk of your different VLs."

"Okay. Synth. The data disk for a VL game."

"Game?" Tag yelled at me. "VL is not a game. It's your digital life. Many people believe your virtual life is more real than 'real life.' Don't disrespect people out there, Mr. Cruz."

"I didn't mean—"

"That's like calling your Ford Pony a hovercar."

"Ouch! That hurts." Now, I understood.

It took two hours for Tag to straighten me out on the language of the virtual reality world. It was divided into two camps—the hardcore gamers, and the lifers, those who lived their lives in VL.

"Is The Five Rings of Babel making money?" I asked.

"It must be, but no one would want the rights to that old synth. It's ancient, now."

"What about Beta Max? He's big time, isn't he?"

"Not really, compared to others. His company is like in the middle third, not a megacorp VL producer, and not one of those making VL out of the trunk of their hovercar. He's a middle player. It's the only way everyone would agree on his being the head of the VRA."

"How long has he been president?"

"Like 12 years."

"Tell me your favorite synths, and why."

It was my way of letting Tag talk with glee about the VR worlds he spent most of his waking hours in. He did. You could see the enthusiasm in his face, the twinkle in his eye. To me, he was sitting up in his darkened room for hours, days, and weeks on end. To him, he got to travel to different lands through time and the universe.

He was a treasure trove of information. Phishy had found me the right kid. My instincts about Beta Max's frantic call were right on target. He was lying, and the only question was whether it was his or the Dame's handiwork.

The real gem I got from Tag was that Beta Max was the President of the Virtual Reality Association. I'd thought it was for his VR empire that she'd wanted him, but after conversing with Tag, learned there was no empire after all, compared to others. However, as President of the VRA, he had *access* to every VR world on the market, and any new one, before it was released to the masses. That market wasn't only Metropolis; it was worldwide, and Up-Top too.

That's why the Dame had him.

CHAPTER 60

Beta Max

"Cruz!" Sidewalk Sally Jane yelled. "What is this all about?"

"We have to get out of here fast," I said back.

The three of us slipped out, down a back-way, and were running to the parking lot of the Liquid Cool building. They were still mad at me for going to the Emporium, and not confronting the NeuroDancer.

"Why didn't you confront her about what she hired you for in the first place that day?" Sidewalk Sally Jane asked me.

"Because that's what she wants me to do, or that's the logical thing to do. I'm not going to beat her by doing the expected. Besides, all she would have to do is lie. How would I know different? I still have no memory of it, and I've done everything I know how to do to try to remember.

"I learned what I came to find out. Am I still under her control? I don't need you two to tell me. Yes, so, let's beat my arch-villain nemesis, before she gets me to do something worse than the last time."

"You're playing with fire, with her," my other sidewalk sally said. "She knows you're after her. Why do you keep playing the game?"

"As long as we're playing the game, I can still catch her. Cockiness and superiority are the trademark fatal flaws of all arch-villains."

"Did you get that from comic book world?" Sidewalk Sally Jane asked, unamused by my responses.

"Well, yeah," I replied, "and 50 years of profile studies of criminal masterminds and psychopathic killers. Be worried when she's not interested in playing anymore. Then we're in trouble."

We burst into the parking lot area. It was a natural blind spot—no lighting, nearly pitch-black. I crouched down in the darkness with my two sidewalk sally bodyguards, as we were joined by another person. This other person looked exactly like me, dressed from head to toe, in a tan fedora and slicker. They got into the Pony, and, in moments, flew out of the parking lot.

If I needed confirmation that I was being followed everywhere, it looked as if at least three different hovercars flew out, too. Maybe it was a coincidence, but I didn't believe so. Regardless, my two sidewalk sallies and Phishy—doing a great job impersonating me—would keep them busy for a long time.

I kept low to the ground. My eyes had now acclimated to the lack of light, and I moved to a hovervan. I gave the back door a tap, and it opened. Inside was Dot's boss from Eye Candy, and three other people. I climbed in and closed the door. Prima Donna locked it.

"I always wanted to be involved in a caper," she said, happy as could be.

"We're like secret agents!" It was Cyan, who had a million outfits—all the same color of cyan.

"Yeah!" The third woman was Goat-Girl, another Eye Candy colleague. She wore a large ring hanging from her nose septum.

"This is Face," Prima Donna said, introducing the man with them. The man was wearing a black turtleneck outfit and was bald as a melon. He had to be good at something for Prima to hire a bald guy at her premiere salon, where hair was king.

"Are you ready?" she asked me.

"Ready. How long will it take?"

"It will take as long as it takes. It's been a while since I did this kind of job." They moved me to the other end of the van, where there was a barber's chair. "But it won't be too long."

When I looked in the mirror after they were done, I couldn't believe it. If I didn't know it was me, I would have sworn it wasn't. I looked completely different. Cyan did my hair. Goat-Girl did the manicuring, then made my hands look very different with makeup. Face, using makeup and small prosthetics, changed the look of my face, down to the bone structure. Prima Donna did the wardrobing, fitting me in an Up-Top style suit, and added colored eye contacts. Now, I had blue eyes. She added the final piece—a fancy, and expensive, pair of shades.

"Why hello, sir," Prima said. "What might your name be?"

"My name's Mr. Incom," I answered.

I had been lucky up to this point in my private investigation career. I'd had no major or minor run-ins with the drug scene in the city. When I was hanging out on the hovercar racing scene there was surprisingly little of it there, but I was with the collector and connoisseur class, and they were not going to wreck a million-dollar vintage vehicle from being stoned, and they were not going to have anyone near their vehicle who was. So far, no one who'd come into my Liquid Cool offices had a case where I was going to have to crawl around in that world, but if they had, I would have turned down the case, no matter how much they wanted to pay me.

The good news was, that I was not going to be in that world. The bad news was that I was about to crawl around in a world that, even without the drugs, was as close to it as any other. The worse news was that many of the virtual reality junkies were also drug junkies.

I was walking through the dark streets, more like the back alleys. My appointment wasn't for a little while, so I wanted to survey the area, pick up a little of the vibe of the crowd. There was one of them. The man had no nose. It was disgusting, and I made sure I wouldn't walk anywhere near him or his cyberpunk buddies, all of them hanging on the street corner smoking. He had no nose because the drugs he snorted had made it decay and fall off. It was common in the drug world.

It was something I never could understand. "No drugs!" wasn't in a moralistic tone with me. It was all about biology. It was playing Russian Roulette with your body and mind. It was like me walking into a bar with my omega-gun and asking aloud who'd let me put my gun to their head and pull the trigger. I'd swear that, since I'd forgotten how many times I'd actually fired it, there was a good chance it was empty. There would be no volunteers.

No doctor, no bio-chemist could tell you if you had the addictive gene in your makeup. Maybe. Maybe not. In my case, I already knew I did—hello, I was a germophobe with OCD tendencies. These idiots were playing Russian Roulette with their brains. We all knew people who "tried it," didn't like it, and then never used it again ever in their life. We all knew occasional users, who lived life fine. We all also knew people who never took a drug in their life, until that fateful moment, and were now some dope roach on the corner, or dead. You could replace every part of your body with a bionic part, except the brain. Don't mess with that brain. Here I was on some nameless mean street with scores of people who disagreed with me. I was passing through; they were permanent fixtures, but they didn't care, which was the problem.

The street I was on had one arcade bar after another. Inside would be VR terminals, where the main player or players jacked-in, and others could too, as spectators. This was what these VR cyberpunks did all day long. Living in VR worlds, drinking their booze, poppin' their blue pill drugs. This was life for them.

I went from one arcade bar to another. All were the same, dark, dank, some smelly, everyone drinking, everyone drugged out, all jacked-in. There were lines of people in front their consoles, most standing, some on high stools; many of the main players were comfortable in recliners. Some parts of the arcades had open cots for people to crash on and get some sleep. They did all kinds of other things, too, in those cot areas.

I was able to tolerate one arcade bar out of all of them. It was a higher-end bar among all the scummy arcade bars. I wouldn't even touch a jack-in helmet with my gloved hands. Thanks to Tag, I had my own equipment. Simple VR glasses with ear pieces. I wouldn't get the real VR experience, but I'd be able to peek into the VR world, and see what the adventure, game, or event was.

The crowd I was with were jacked-in to a worldwide martial arts kill-fest. In their VR world, the goal was simple: beat everyone else you encountered to death, grab all the money, and grab all the members of the opposite sex (or whatever else you were into). It was all laughs and yelling with this group.

There were much more cultured VR worlds out there, but not here. No cultured culture to be found here—ever. I had wasted enough time. I'd seen what I wanted, and continued up the street.

It was always fascinating to walk down a street and watch the neighborhoods change. I never understood how that happened. Cross a line, and you'd go from grimy and slimy, to decent and presentable, to upscale, upper-crust. How did people manage this?

I walked just a few feet, and immediately, the area was different. Instead of cyberpunk riff-raff, I was with the cyberpunk geeks. These were the kids. Their arcade bars were more juvenile, just as loud, but there were more beers, and juice alcohols, than the super hard drinks where I'd come from. I moved to VR worlds of all sex and violence, to ones of fighting dragons in dungeons, spaceship races through the galaxy, or hunting aliens on jungle planets in other galaxies and times. It was a much different vibe, and I ended up spending more time here than I had anticipated.

The next big change in areas was when I crossed over into the VL-ers (VEE-LERS). These were the people that "lived" in virtual reality. These were not arcade bars. Virtual lifers congregated in these dens where people sat in ultra-plush recliners, and the jack-in interface wasn't helmets or glasses; it was a full-body capsule over the person. The non-initiated, like me, called them VR coffins. There was no rowdiness here. The only sounds heard were hundreds of conversations.

I jacked into one group. At first, I had to comprehend what was going on. These virtual lifers were in Metropolis—but it was their own virtual version of Metropolis. There was no rain, no griminess. I saw the sun above in a bright blue sky, white billowy clouds, birds, even. Everything looked so clean and spotless. People were not in grays and blacks, but whites and bright colors. It was beautiful.

I unjacked myself immediately. That was a VR world I had to stay away from. That was potentially too addictive for me. I looked on one of their chair consoles to see the name of the VR world. I committed the name of the synth to memory. Yes, stay the hell away from this VR world. I was a red-pill believer in real reality. No blue-pill worlds of bliss for me.

One common establishment next to these arcade bars and VR dens were massage parlors, with their own VR beds.

"Get your Swedish here!"

"Get your Chinese here!"

"Naked massage, while you travel through a land of bliss. Ooo la la!" the computer voices repeated.

Naked massage with some stranger roaming around below. Oh no no!

I wasn't sure if the place we were meeting at was a hotel, or bar, or both, but Beta Max was waiting for me outside the door.

"Mr. Incom!" He was flanked by a young woman in neon clothing on each side. He shook my hand vigorously, and then put an arm on my shoulder as he led me inside.

"I'm so glad to finally meet you. We'll go right in here. Can I have a drink, or any food brought in?"

"Thank you, but no," I replied.

"Hope you don't mind if I do."

"Not at all."

He spoke to the two women, and they left us. Beta Max took me through what looked to be a bar-nightclub ground floor. We went up a flight of short stairs and into a large office space. Two large guards in suits stood outside the door. Inside, there were only two chairs and a small table in between. One wall had a display screen, where one commercial after another flashed onto different VR worlds, on mute.

"Have a seat, Mr. Incom. Again, I'm so glad to be meeting with you."

"I was told you were the man to meet," I said.

The two women returned with food and drinks for Beta Max.

"I brought these, in case you change your mind, sir," one of them said to me, and set a plate, chopsticks, and a glass of blue alcohol on the table.

The two women left us again. Beta Max had already finished half his drink, and set the glass on the table.

"Mr. Incom, I have to confess, I've never been paid so much money simply to talk to someone about a business proposal, but this is Metropolis; theres a first for everything."

"Mr. Max, can we talk? I mean, is this room secure."

"Completely. I have it swept daily, and those bodyguards outside the door never leave it unattended."

"You're very Egyptian, Mr. Max."

"How so?"

"You control the entire pyramid. The masses below and the wealthy at the pinnacle. Smart business model."

Beta Max was just a smiling fool.

"Mr. Incom, I see I'm speaking to a man who can appreciate big picture planning."

"I'll get straight to it. My company, and I'm sure you checked out both my company and me thoroughly, are not looking to simply do business with you. We are looking for a joint-business partner. We don't view you as simply the president of an industry association. We view you in larger terms. You are a VL evangelist. A cybervangelist. In your role, you are in a unique vantage point."

"As VRA's president, it's a balancing act. I can't profit at all from my position. I see the latest virtual worlds before the public, but so does the VL media."

"No, Mr. Max. We're not primarily interested in profit. We're interested in power. You have that access; we have the capital. We're not interested in the VR worlds. We're interested in their users, here on Earth and off-world. You already have the access here in Metropolis, and have been expanding across the planet. We want to help you get the rest of the way, with our financing and Up-Top contacts. Are you interested, Mr. Max?"

The look on Beta Max's face was like someone who was trying to contain his exuberance at winning the Metro Lotto. He was fighting with himself, to keep from jumping up from his seat and screaming.

Calmly, he said, "I am."

Beta Max was no doofus. It was an act. He purposely wanted people—the wrong people—to think less of him.

We had left that establishment, and went by hoverlimo to one of his factories. It was located in Silver City, so even his offices being in low-town Free City were a ruse. He was a booshy, uptown business mogul, like every other working in the wealthy Silver City, a place that, after my Case of the Blade Gunner, I had no burning interest to return to, but here we were again. Its allure wasn't the fact that it was the heart of the robotics production of Metropolis. It was one of the most secure sections of the city, especially after the recent incident that'd happened here (yes, my Case of the Blade Gunner again).

Beta Max was the man in charge now. He gave me the platinum tour of the facility.

"You employ all these cyberpunks?" I asked.

He laughed. "Cyberpunk doesn't mean what it used to mean. Computer tech geeks, hacker hooligans, and VR junkies. The average toddler on this planet can be considered a computer tech geek. Hacking done by some youngster in their basement might have been true in the distant past, but not now. Analog technology is so sophisticated, and the physical safeguards paradoxically are so rudimentary, only the hacking teams of hundreds, at only the largest megacorps have even the remotest chance of breaching government or corporate systems. VR junkies? Yes, that one I agree with, but that's why we hired them. We're a VR firm, so who best to play, program, and perfect?"

I watched the endless cubicles of jacked-in kids using virtual keyboards.

"They don't seem to be playing or programming. They're typing data."

"Fifty percent of the country is Asian. Sixty percent of the total population is classified as some level of cyborg. Ten percent are super wealthy. The number we like is 90—90 percent use VR. Only 30 percent are the hardcore users. Add occasional users and you add the other 60 percent. All in virtual reality.

"That's a lot of data. Centuries ago, we could collect data on what people liked to buy, eat, how much money they made, where they lived, have lived, would live, who they voted for, who they were married to, who they were dating, who they wished they were dating, who they were attracted to, how many kids they had, where they went for vacation, what movies they liked, what books they read. Now, for the first time in human history, we can know what they think and desire. With that knowledge, we're not influencing anymore, as in the past; we are able to control."

I nodded. "Mr. Max, it's exactly that kind of strategic thinking that makes my company want to partner with you. In fact, we want you to run the effort. How do you do it, Mr. Max?"

"That, Mr. Incom, is our secret sauce. If you knew that, you wouldn't need me."

"That's precisely why we want to partner with you. In broad strokes, walk me through it. I've heard everything from HCI, the old neural interface, to BCI and neural manipulation."

"You've been reading up."

"The wild rantings of the tech and VR media. We know all they've written is false, but what's false for many, doesn't have to be false for a few."

"I have a feeling you're going to tell me you've been watching me," Beta Max said.

"When a mid-level VR architect, at best, is 'inquiring' about VR firms Up-Top, we got curious."

"A colleague of mine told me I shouldn't have done that."

"You shouldn't have. It indicates your greediness. Greed leads to impatience, and then mistakes. That's why we made our generous contribution to you. You don't have to be greedy anymore. We'll gladly feed that beast. No impatience, no mistakes. If any other megacorp, Up-Top, or even the government of Metropolis suspected it—"

"Yes, I know."

"Give me the broad strokes, Mr. Max."

"Oh." Max got his mind back on track. "Human-computer interface is ancient history, Mr. Incom. VR body jacks disappeared around the same time as those cranial hard-drives. They weren't called brain-melters on the street for nothing. Neural interfaces have promise, but are still nothing more than clip-on, external microcircuitry jewelry for lab rats, at this point. The EEG technology of BCI is the standard. But as you know, brain computer interface is not telekinesis. The only neural manipulations we can do is brainwave to computer, and not the other way around.

"What are your favorite VR worlds, Mr. Incom?"

I knew it was a test. He was suspicious of me all of a sudden.

"I'm partial to Vinyl River and Amber Ladder myself, with a bit of techno salsa in the background."

Beta Max laughed.

"What are your favorite VR worlds, Mr. Max?"

"I'll always have a special place in my heart for The Five Rings of Babel, but hovercycling in Neon Jungle is my favorite. So, Mr. Incom, I realize now that we may have been having a conversation all this time, but we may have been on different pages."

Max was backtracking now.

I handed him a mini-tablet. He played it, and the smile disappeared from his face. "Did you employ a Metropolis private detective named Cruz?"

He hesitated. "If you're asking about him by name, you know I did."

"That video shows him throwing himself off a roof, which would have been successful had it not been for those two people who came after him. Mr. Max, this is very important. I'm about to reveal something most on Earth don't know. There are two VR firms battling secretly to bring to market a VR world that can—control the actions and behaviors of its users. Mr. Max, if we were to partner and finance you, just you, no partners, no matter how much it takes, could you bring such a VR world to market first?"

There was poker, and there was the poker of life. Beta Max was already suspicious of me for some reason. He stared at me, sizing me up, for the longest time. I could see the debate raging within himself.

"Should we take our money elsewhere?" I poked him with the final verbal dagger.

"No," Beta Max responded quickly this time.

He took me to his Silver City offices—his real office, not the Free City one. Beta Max was leaning on his fancy glass desk with neon trim.

"In the past, we had roboticists and futurists saying that Artificial Intelligence was impossible, then, when it was, it would never evolve past the state of a retarded cockroach, then it would evolve to true sentience and take over the world. People have made many bold announcements and products since then, and what they've tried to trick us with haven't been retarded cockroaches, but dumb cockroaches.

"VR has shown us the way, though. Why try to copy the human brain in a computer, machine, or robot? Especially when you have such a popular anti-robot union movement and sentiment in the city. Forget the machines. Just control the humans with the brains."

I had him. He was my rat in my maze.

"Mr. Max, what do you call the process? Mind control is not what it is."

He smiled. "I call it 'neuro-sorcery.'"

How did NeuroDancer "zombie" me and so many others? Beta Max gave me the term. It was the singular word that stuck in my mind and sent a shiver down my spine the second he said it.

It was time for me to return the favor.

CHAPTER 61

Mr. Incom

What did I have? Nothing.

I knew a lot, but it wasn't enough. 'Neuro-sorcery.' I had the word, but nothing more. Beta Max had done a lot of talking, but thinking about what he'd said, I hadn't gotten what I needed to fill in the blanks. I still didn't know how.

The two women had taken me back down the elevator capsule, and through the lobby to the private parking bay of the building. Beta Max wanted to come, but I gave him an assignment: get the papers drawn up with his attorneys, and we'd solidify the partnership to begin. In other words, I was stalling for time. I knew he was on his phone with his attorneys.

As we were walking to the private parking bay doors, a group of suits came through, and passed us.

I stopped in the hallway, and they looked back at me.

"Excuse me," I called out to them.

The group of men stopped, too. "Yes," one of them said to me.

"May I ask what company you're with?"

They laughed, and the man said, "Sir, your mother raised you with far too many manners. Of course you may. Don't you see the name on our badges?"

I stepped forward and stared at the badges. I felt my forehead sweating.

"This may sound strange, but I suffer from an affliction that makes me unable to see text sometimes."

The suits looked at each other. The man looked at his badge, looked at me, and then pointed at his badge. "It says, 'V-T-V.' You know what that means."

"The communications conglomerate."

"There you go. So, you have seen us. Who might you be?"

"My name's Incom. My company is unimportant. Thank you, and sorry for the inconvenience."

"It was no inconvenience, sir."

The suits left, and I turned to my two escorts. One of them was on her phone, and she immediately flicked it off. I'd already seen on the video screen who it was—Beta Max.

I smiled. They didn't.

"Tell Mr. Max that this is where I leave the story."

I pushed past them out the bay doors before they even had a chance to react. Alarms sounded locking all doors, and all elevator capsules began to return to surface level.

One of the women flicked on her mobile phone. "Mr. Incom escaped through the parking bay doors before the lock-down."

"That was not any Mr. Incom!" Beta Max yelled. "That was that detective Cruz in disguise!"

CHAPTER 62

Cyberpunks

Sometimes, that's how a case was wrapped up, by pure luck. Virtual Television, VTV, the communications megacorp: that was the missing piece. That was the final piece!

VTV was how a movie producer-gangster, political adviser-gangster, and VR world producer-ex-gangster were all tied together. Caret wasn't just for the money; he had the movie content. Logo wasn't just for the politicians; he was for the government contacts. Beta Max was the gateway to the means to *everyone:* A VTV in the home of every man, woman, and child in Metropolis. No wonder Beta Max was like a hog in slop at what I was proposing. In his mind, I was telling him there would be a VTV in the home of every man, woman, and child on Earth, and off-world, all the way to Mars.

I'd known the Dame's plan was diabolical, but never really the full scope of it until then.

I ran out of there so fast. Thanks to my previous visits to the place, from my last case, and when I was on the hovercar racing scene, I knew how to escape Silver City unseen. They could have sent an army of robo-tracking dogs after me. I was gone.

When I got to Police One, I saw on the newsfeed screens that Metro FD was out in force in Silver City. A series of explosions had rocked one of the office towers, and hoverfiretrucks were out in force. I knew exactly who it was. Beta Max was destroying the evidence. They were going to make sure there was nothing left for us to find.

That was fine because I didn't come to Police One to get the Calvary for Silver City. For once, I was going to be a step ahead of them.

We were at VRA headquarters. The Virtual Reality Association building was some hole-in-the-wall mini-tower of 50 stories at the very edge of Buzz Town, not far from my Liquid Cool offices. I pushed the buzzer outside their locked main front door, and some kid's face appeared.

"What?" he asked.

"Is that how you professionally answer the door to a potential customer?" I asked. I was back in "uniform"—tan fedora, tan slicker, and my normal dress. I was Cruz again.

The kid jerked his head back in a grimace, thinking. "Yeah."

"Who's in charge there? Because it surely isn't you."

"Whatever, bro."

"Get the person in charge now, or we're breaking down the front door."

He noticed the police with me. The kid was now scared, and disappeared from the screen. Another kid's face appeared, with what was trying to be a mustache on his face. "Who are you?"

"My name is Cruz. I'm a private detective."

"Oh, yeah. I know you. I bought one of your T-shirts on the Net. Dude, those T-shirts suck. Where were they made? They really do suck. Your picture on them fades after a few washes."

"With me," I continued, ignoring the kid, "is Chief of Police Hub, one of his captains, known as The Wrecker, you can look at him yourself to see why, a dozen street officers, and half a dozen CSI agents."

"What the hell?"

"If you get on the keyboard, and immediately send out a notice to your entire membership right now that Beta Max is no longer the President of the VRA, pending a criminal investigation by the Metro DA, we'll come in, verify it, and go. If you don't, we'll break down the door, seize every computer and device in there, place you under arrest, that other kid under arrest, everyone else in there—human, pet and robot."

We heard voices all around him, and the kid said, "I'm buzzing you in now. Don't get all police brutality on us. We believe in peace not war—"

"Open the door!" I yelled.

"Buzzing."

PART EIGHT

Smoking Rooms, Booze Bottles, and Laser Guns

CHAPTER 63

Caret

I had smashed all of them! We were entering the dangerous period. When I was a police intern as a kid, they told us all kinds of stories of criminals doing everything possible to cover their tracks, get rid of their contraband, and prepare for their escape. One criminal killed all his gangster partners; he was so afraid they'd flip, and testify against him. Another tried to whack his own wife, positive she'd turned city evidence. Another burned tens of millions of his drug product, so Narco couldn't get it; the only problem was the drug fumes knocked him out, and he ended up almost burning himself up. NeuroDancer was going to go into clean-up mode too: eliminate all loose ends before disappearing. The race was in its final stretch.

Caret was his wild and crazy self, commanding all the attention at the high-stakes card game.

"Jokers, boys! When the jokers are wild, I get wild. Wild and crazy. Give me them jokers, so I can take your money!"

"Not this time, Caret," one of the thugs at the table said. "I gotcha beat this time."

The pot in the center was overflowing with money.

"What you got? You can't beat me. Didn't your mother tell you?"

"Tell me what, Caret?"

"I am your father!"

The men at the table laughed.

"Funny, Caret, but I've still got you beat."

"Show me what you've got."

The thug threw down his hand. "There! I told ya!"

Caret held his hand close and looked at them. "Why does everyone think they're some kind of joker?" Caret threw down his winning cards.

The card crew went wild.

"Pal, you will never beat me. I am your master."

"Caret, one day, I'll figure out how you cheat so good."

"Cheat? Who needs cheating, when the jokers are wild!"

"Boss," a young man came to the table, "you've got some new challengers. They want the next game."

Caret looked at the bar, where a few men stood.

"New challengers. Well, come on down!"

"Where are you boys from?" Caret asked, dealing the cards.

"I'm from Metropolis," one man said, taking his cards.

"Me, I'm from Metropolis."

"Metropolis," the third man said, also grabbing his cards.

"Just passing through the galaxy," the fourth man said.

Caret laughed. "Passing through the galaxy? From Up-Top?"

"Been there. Been here. Just around." The man was clearly not the conversationalist type.

"Boys, jokers are wild in this game. I'm giving you advance warning. When the jokers are wild, I get wild. Wild and crazy. If I get them jokers, I'll take your money!"

The men managed laughs.

"Why so uptight, boys? You're not drinking. You're not laughing at my jokes. Why so serious?"

"We're here to play cards."

"Play cards without the show. What's the fun in that?"

"As I said, we're here to play cards, and win some money."

"Are you packing?" Caret asked, with a smile.

The question made them all take pause.

"Packing?" the fourth man asked.

"Is it a big gun?"

"I don't carry guns."

"You don't carry any guns? That's no fun."

"Guns and cards don't mix, in my experience," the third man interjected.

"Sometimes they don't. Sometimes they do," Caret said, dealing the next hand.

"Don't you make movies?" the second man asked.

"There we go! The conversation is here. Now, we got a real card game. Yeah, I make movies. Lots of them. I love making me some movies."

"What's your favorite kind of movies to make?" the second man asked.

"Wait a minute." Caret pointed at the first man. "Where's the conversation? Are you going to give me some love?"

"Tell us about the main themes and allegorical metaphors you explore in your films," he asked.

Caret hit the top of the card table with a palm. "That's what I'm talking about! This is a card game! Conversation, the con, convicts, and killers!

"What are my favorite movies to make? First question first. Space operas! I love 'em. Good guys saving princesses from other planets. Really bad guys with baritone voices, alien powers, cyborg bodies. Then you can get those cool space battles and blow stuff up! Sound can't travel in the void of space, but all my movies—Bam! I want to blow out people's eardrums with those explosions in space."

"What did you mean when you said 'con, convicts, and killers,'?" the fourth man asked.

Caret leaned over and slapped his right hand. "Don't interrupt. I'm answering questions and telling interesting movie stories.

"Where was I? Main themes and allegorical metaphors in my films. Great question. Lot of meat on that question. The good guy and the bad guy are always related somehow. Best friends in school, brothers, father and son, something. Metaphorically, it says good comes from evil and evil comes from good, or something like that. I like that Eastern religion stuff. In Western religion, good and evil are separate, and good always triumphs over evil—Boring! The bad never goes away. Yesterday's bad guy is tomorrow's good guy. Yeah! I like that.

"Then you gotta get that skin and nakedness in there somewhere for the 18-to-40 demographic. Very important. You can't get any kind of bad movie made nowadays without that."

Caret turned to the fourth man. "Okay, Mr. Rude Man, interrupting my train of thought mojo, and not waiting his turn. What was your question? Oh, yeah! Con, convicts and killers! That's not what I said. I said: Conversation, the con, convicts, and killers!

"We've got the conversation now! The con is, you boys are the worst card players ever. I knew before you sat down you don't play cards.

Convicts? That's you. Killers, that's the guys you have all around this bar!—and you, too."

The four men rose from their seats in unison, and attempted to pull guns from their jackets. Caret fired his laser gun from under the table where he sat, and shot all four of the thugs dead.

The bar exploded in a gun fight. Men shooting at him, Caret's men shooting back. Laser blasts flew everywhere.

"Well, this is plain crazy," Caret said to himself, stood up and flew, via jetpack, to the second floor.

When he landed, he noticed one of the hitmen after him had an amazing, samurai-style—but super-illegal—laser sword (a red laser beam along the edge, emitting from the tip to the hilt of the sword). "Where do they get such wonderful toys?" he said to himself, and then he ran off.

Moments later, he jumped back down with a huge laser pulse machine gun and mowed down all the hitmen.

One of Caret's men ran up to him. "Boss, we got the ones outside."

"Well, that's good to know. I was actually more concerned about the ones right here, who were doing the actual direct shooting at me."

Caret walked over to one of the dead hitmen, and grabbed the laser sword from his hand. "I don't think you'll be needing this anymore."

"Who tried to whack you, boss?" Caret's man asked.

"Who else but Logo?"

"Boss!" Another man appeared with a mobile in his hand.

"Yes," Caret said. "What is it?"

"You have a call. He says his name is Cruz."

Caret smiled as he stared at my face on the display.

"Mr. Cruz, this is an unexpected surprise."

"I heard you had some hitman trouble," I said.

"How could you know that, Mr. Cruz, when it happened—like now?"

"My people have been keeping tabs on you; that's how. But that's not why I'm calling. The person who tried to have you killed was not Logo."

"Why do you say that, Mr. Cruz?"

"Because someone tried to kill him five minutes ago, too. I know it wasn't you."

"Interesting."

"The same person who tried to kill him, tried to kill you."

"Who might that be?"

"His name is Beta Max."

"Hmm. I don't know who that is, Mr. Cruz."

"You knew him by a slightly different name. Here's his photo."

Beta Max's static photo replaced my live video display.

"Oh," Caret said. "I haven't seen that face in a while. I knew we should have killed him back then."

CHAPTER 64

Logo

Japan Jamaica was the bar. It was a long-time establishment in the nouveau-riche part of Neon Blues that catered to old Japanese businessmen, and new Japanese cyberpunks.

Logo sat by himself in a secluded section of the bar, enjoying the karaoke performance. Karaoke in Japan Jamaica was always by up-and-coming, soon-to-be-famous dance singers. There was never anything amateur about a performance in Japan Jamaica. On the side table was his glass of Japanese whiskey. On both sides, behind him, against the wall were two bodyguards, arms clasped in front, emotionless and quiet.

His young son appeared, got his father's attention, and nodded.

Several gray-haired men sat with him, booze and smokes in hand.

"We decided on the kid," one man said.

"Who?" Logo asked.

"Ito. We like him. He's presentable. Attractive family. Paid his dues. Controllable."

"Ito will be good."

"The megacorps have decided on their handpicked candidate too."

"Who?" Logo asked.

"Moto. We hate him. He looks like a dog's backside. Disrespectful. Doesn't honor the old ways."

"Moto would be bad."

"How can you guarantee Ito will beat their person?"

"Have I ever not delivered?"

"Sorry," the man said.

"Money."

The man placed his cigarette to hang from the side of his mouth, and put his drink on the table. He passed a paper bag around the men, and each one put in fat wads of cash. He stood and pulled a wad from his jacket and put it in the bag.

Logo pointed to the side table near him, and the man put down the bag. The man half shook his hand, and then did a traditional Japanese bow. All the men got up, each doing the same before following, leaving the section, and then the bar.

With a simple hand gesture, one of the bodyguards behind him took the bag of money and disappeared. A waitress appeared, and refilled his half-empty glass. He noticed his son in the distance again, looking directly at him.

Logo simply stared at him.

His son neared him and leaned down to whisper something in his ear.

The hovercars, souped-up with flashing neon bumper and side trim, flew into the Japan Jamaica bar parking bay one after another, seven in all. Security—big, beefy, cyborgs—stopped each one separately to check them out.

"You got a reservation?" the cyborg security guard asked.

"No, brother, we're just getting some drinks for the girls and coming to see a show."

The security guard noticed in the backseats were scantily clad women.

"Okay, go on in." He waved the first one through, and the guards ended up doing the same for the other six hovercars, though only the first three had females—the rest had all males.

They parked next to each other—each with a different flashing neon color. All the men exited, but the women stayed in the hovercars.

Logo sat in his chair, enjoying the karaoke performance. On the side table was his glass of Japanese whiskey and a laser rapier—a sword with a long, quarter-inch thin lighted blade. Behind him, all along the wall, were ten bodyguards, arms folded, emotionless and quiet.

The hitmen were digital samurai—the street name for enforcers, who used laser swords patterned after Up-Top technology. The sword weapons were metal rods with switch-on laser blades.

The first one pushed a button on his collar, and green cyber-tattoos appeared on his face as he flicked on dark shades. All his compatriots following him did the same.

The bartenders began firing first, and then the waitresses next—automatic pistols. Patrons and karaoke singers dived for cover. The digital samurai attacked.

The ten bodyguards behind Logo stepped forward to attack, but did not need to act. Most of the digital samurai were cut down by Japan Jamaica staff.

The remaining digital samurai ran at Logo. One threw his laser blade at him, but the gangster sidestepped, dodging it. Logo killed the weaponless hitman with his laser-rapier first, then engaged the other two.

The sword fight went on for a few minutes.

"Enough!" Logo yelled. He spun around to slice and bayonet the men. Logo was red with anger.

"How did this happen?" he yelled at his son, who approached his father.

"Logo!" a man appeared from a back room. "A gang shootout in my bar!"

"Yes, think of all the new customers you'll get now," Logo said.

He pointed into the chest of his son. "How did this happen?"

The son gestured to other men. "Protect Mr. Logo with your life!" He looked at his father. "I'll have the scene secure."

"Get the money!" Logo yelled.

The son ran to the guards along the wall.

"Logo!" the owner yelled. "The police will be here in three minutes!"

Logo's son appeared with the bag of money.

"Get out of here before the police arrive," Logo said to him.

"Logo! Am I getting some of that money?" the owner asked.

"I will take care of you. I always do," Logo said to the owner.

"You've got seven neon hovercars outside!" the son yelled at them. "You'll be able to sell them for restitution!"

"Go!" Logo said to him.

The boy ran with the bag of money. The guards tightened their circle around Logo, waiting for the police.

"Logo!" the owner yelled.

"What!" Logo replied.

"There's a Cruz on the phone for ya."

Logo walked to the bar video-phone with his guards.

He stared at my face on the bar's video-phone display.

"Mr. Cruz, you are catching me at an inconvenient time. How did you know I was here?"

"I've had my people watching you for days."

"Days? I didn't know you had people, Mr. Cruz."

"Yeah, you can always tell them. They're the ones wearing Liquid Cool T-shirts."

Logo smiled. "This call will be a short one." I could hear the sirens.

"Did you just have some hitman trouble?" I asked.

"Your people keep you well informed, Mr. Cruz."

"Do you know who did it?"

"Mr. Cruz, I believe we've had previous conversations about a man named Caret."

"It wasn't him. In fact, as soon as you get out of Metro PD, call him."

"Why would I do that, Mr. Cruz?"

"Don't you want to live long, prosper, and all that? Because the person who just tried to kill you sent a team to kill him too. It's going on now. You don't want Caret."

"Who do I want, Mr. Cruz?"

"A man named Beta Max."

"I don't know any such person, Mr. Cruz."

Beta Max's static photo replaced my live video display.

Logo had a frown on his face. "T-Ron."

"Yes," I said. "You and Caret should talk."

CHAPTER 65

Beta Max

Beta Max sat in his private Free City office alone, wearing VR goggles. In the VR world, he took turns jumping between the Palace, and Japan Jamaica Bar. He watched the police on the ground, police cruisers in the air, hoverambulances, medics, police investigators, the crowds congregating behind cordon lines. All of Metropolis could be experienced in virtual reality.

He had to know. He wanted to see the bodies of his former rivals carried out on hovergurneys.

"Where are they?" he asked to himself.

He switched to split screen: the Palace Bar was on the left field of view, and Japan Jamaica on the right. The newsfeed audio was going wild with speculation. Whether true or not, everyone listened. People always listened and gossiped.

"Tell me something," he said to himself. "Give me names."

"We're talking about two different gangland shootouts at approximately the same time," one reporter said.

"Police have not confirmed if these are coordinated events, or completely separate," another media person's voice said.

"Why do you think they're coordinated?" Beta Max asked himself. "You don't know that. Why are you saying that? I know they're coordinated. You don't. Give me the news I want to hear!"

"Max!"

He heard his secretary call out on the intercom. At first, he ignored her, but she kept calling. He pulled off the goggles.

"What?" he yelled.

"You have three calls!"

"I said, 'Hold all calls!'"

"Caret and Logo are holding."

Beta Max looked at the video-phone with a scared expression.

"Who's on the third line?" he yelled.

"Some guy named Cruz. He said you hired him."

Beta Max picked up the call. He was smiling even before my face appeared on the display screen.

"Cruz!"

"Save the act," I said. "They know."

"They know. Who knows? What are you talking about?"

"Keep playing games. They know you sent the hitmen after them, because I called them afterward, and told them it was you. Your little scam to make them each think the other did it is blown. I thought you should know." I hung up.

Beta Max jumped up from his chair and ran to the office door. Beta Max threw the door open.

"Get out of here!" he yelled at the secretary. "Now! Take the back way! The real back way!"

"What's happening?" She jumped up from her desk.

He ran to the file cabinet, opening it, and threw something to her. It was a gun.

"What about you?" she asked.

"Get out of here, now! I'll take care of me!"

The secretary ran to the door, hesitated, jumped to the side before throwing it open. A big man in black, with a body canopy attached to his shoulders, stood at the doorway. Beta Max fired at him, the man fired back, and the secretary fired at the man from the side. The stranger fell to the ground.

"Run!" Beta Max yelled.

She bolted down the hallway. Beta Max grabbed things from the cabinet, then ran into the hall too, but was met by laser gun-fire. He threw himself back into the office for cover.

Three men, also with body canopies attached at their shoulders, ran down the hall to the office. When they reached the doorway—darkness. Every light in the office and the hallway went out. They couldn't see anything. Three laser blasts fired, and all three fell back to the ground, dead.

Beta Max, with his VR goggles on, ran back into the hallway with a box of things in one hand and ran. He didn't need light with his goggles.

The parking lot was in the middle of the tower, and accessible by stairs. He ran down two flights in the pitch dark, and came out the door. They couldn't see him, but there was a virtual army of men around his hover mini-van. Some gang he had never seen before, who all wore body canopies. Body canopies were worn to keep the rain off you without wearing a hood, hat or using an umbrella. For these punks, it was their "uniform."

"Who's there?" one yelled. "Answer us!"

They started firing in the direction of the door.

Beta Max, crouching close to the ground, opened the box, pulled out a pen-like device and pressed a button on it. The hover mini-van powered on, rose in the air. Beta Max, via remote control, took his time to run over and crush every last punk. Some tried to run, some tried to crawl away.

Beta Max flew out of the parking garage in his hover mini-van as quickly as he could. Almost as quickly, he set down nearby, shut it off, and ran into the night, pulling off his goggles. He didn't have much time.

Caret and Logo would be coming for him, and he had to get ready.

I was playing a very dangerous game.

Now, I had three gangsters playing Cops and Robbers on the streets of Metropolis, with live guns. Caret and Logo would be at Metro Central for a while, but not forever. They both had fancy lawyers and even gangsters were allowed to defend themselves from getting murdered in a public place. There was no sense trying to follow them. The second they were released by police, they would vanish. They were going to find Beta Max, and kill him. I needed Beta Max alive. Actually, I needed all three of them alive.

The only chance I had to make that happen was to find where Beta Max was going to hide himself. There was no doubt in my mind that Caret and Logo's combined forces—yeah, the former rivals were going to be like a married couple from this day forward, until they put Beta Max in the ground—would easily find his lair. Beta Max thought he was good; Caret and Logo were better.

I needed to find Beta Max first and then wait. I hopped into the Pony, with my two sidewalk sally bodyguards, and we were gone. Out there in Metropolis there was a mini-gang war about to go down.

NeuroDancer was cleaning up all her loose ends, but the men involved didn't even know they were the rats in her dance show.

CHAPTER 66

The Knight, the Captain and the President

It was Caret who had started the House of Jed a long time ago. Back then, it was just called The House, and Caret was a "knight" of the universal force himself. I wasn't sure that being a gangster and running a cult on the side mixed well, but he did it. He left the gangsterism, to become a legitimate businessman, and he turned the House over to others. Later, I found out Jed had started as one of Caret's hoods, so Caret probably was fine leaving the cult, since its management was still in the criminal family. Then the men fell out.

Logo was a gangster, who left the crime biz to be a pilot. He loved to fly, and flew everything on Earth to get the rank of captain, then flew craft in space. Organized crime said he'd left the flying business for the political power broker business, which I didn't know was a business. He was the consigliere, who found people to run for office, to represent specific interests of businesses, though not at the megacorporation level. Logo carved out a nice niche for himself, representing business families and groups that had assets less than the multi-trillion level.

Beta Max, president of the Virtual Reality Association, ex-gangster, now was a VR world software guru. Out of the three, I believed he was the Dame's main man, and not because they were, or had been married. She was going to use VR World technology to take her mind-control *neuro-sorcery* ability big time. I was sure of it. That's why he was her number one.

Everyone would say mind control was impossible, but I was the one who almost did the header off my own office tower's rooftop. I needed these three men. Even if we couldn't get them to talk, which was a strong possibility, just having them would make her nervous. It had to, because nervous criminals became stupid criminals, and a flurry of mistakes would then ensue. That's when you caught them.

Where was Beta Max hiding?

Beta Max knew the danger he was in. He couldn't go home, or to the home of anyone he knew. There was only one safe house—his Shack. Most people didn't know Free City had small ground-level storage sheds. It was a holdover from an earlier era.

Storage sheds today took up floor after floor of the modern monolith tower. He had his own, and used them. Tonight, he needed something that wasn't a huge container; he needed his safe house. He had never said a word out loud, even to his employees, about the Shack. Only one other person knew it existed, but he had to know if she'd turn him in.

A small refrigerator in the corner, a tiny stove and oven, a small, but comfortable twin bed against one wall. It was always cold and damp, so he had to have the heaters running whenever he was there, which wasn't too often. He used the Shack to come up with the next big idea, the next great software idea. He'd come up with the best ones in this Shack: no distractions, no one to bother him, no phones, no TVs. It didn't even have a VR console with screen.

He kept the Shack free of any metal or alloy, free of any electronics. That's what he had in the box he'd grabbed from the office, his portable scanner, to scan for bugs, pieces of metal, or any electric discharge. That was his foolproof way to keep it his ideal sanctuary.

There was a director's chair that he sat in. Since there were no electronics, he couldn't watch a remote video monitor. He had to watch for any uninvited guests physically, and that's what he was doing. The doors of the Shack were wide open. No one knew, because there were no lights above the Shack. There were no lights in the Shack—he only used candles, and plastic light-sticks. It was pitch black inside, but outside, beyond the Shack, there were the busy streets.

The shacks were at one end of Free City that had scarce hovercar traffic, and even scarcer foot traffic. He sat in the dark, waiting. An occasional sigh, the low hum of the heaters behind the chair to keep warm, the light drizzle of the falling rain made most of the noise that his ears picked up. He watched and listened for everything.

There was one other thing the Shack had: it's own secret armory. Across his lap was a military-style pulse rifle. It was so old that it technically wasn't illegal anymore, but it was fully operational, and the power of the weapon was what he needed.

They would either come, or they wouldn't.

If they didn't come, he'd be here all night, until the trash hovertrucks flew by, indicating dawn. He'd pack up, and get out of Metropolis as quickly as he could. It would mean they'd been unable to find him, and would plant themselves at his known spots, which he'd never return to. He'd be out of the supercity forever.

If they came, it would mean she'd told them. It would mean she'd sent the executioners that came. He would never escape Metropolis alive.

At first, they looked like fireflies, but as he stared a bit longer, he could see the two yellow neon hoverbikes approach. They were not on the normal sky lanes but flying free-form. A black hovercar sped by, just above them, and disappeared. The two yellow hoverbikes then did a diagonal descent, then stopped just ten feet from the ground, and then raced back up to the sky in spiraling motions.

They had to be kids, perfecting their riding skills. The pattern was repeated—diagonal descent, and then spiraling back up to about 20 feet. He watched them practice their routines several more times over the course of almost 20 minutes. Sometimes slower, sometimes racing fast. At the end, they stopped on the ground, and he could see the figures of two people, smoking. He couldn't quite make out what they were saying, but they were loud.

A black hovercar sped by again. Was it the same one from before?

Another yellow hoverbiker appeared, and joined the other two on the ground. Now, he could hear laughing. It seemed they were showing off new outfits, as he could see their jackets change colors. He was fixated by the three hoverbike kids. He wished he could hear what they were saying, to pass the time.

He remembered when he had been a kid like they were. Once, he could hang out on the street, on the corner, under a walkway all night long. Back then, time flew by, not like now, sitting in his director's chair, where every second crawled by at sub-light speed.

The rain had completely stopped. He had hoped he'd be able to hear them better now, but they were louder, not more comprehensible. They had turned on the music on their hoverbikes, and that brought laughter and dancing. This could end up being a long night. The music they were playing and dancing to he absolutely hated. Planet metal. Why did they have to be metal heads?

All of a sudden, they got on their hoverbikes, spiraled up, and away.

He jumped. A glass bottle shattered on the ground, right where the hoverbiker kids had been.

A black hovercar sped by, much closer to the ground, this time.

Beta Max, instead of having his weapon on his lap, wrapped his hands around it. Maybe it was nothing. Why would they ride around over and over again if it were them?

Cruz!

That gave him something to pass the time with. That little detective had put him in this situation. But if Cruz hadn't called him, he wouldn't have known. They would have gotten him in his office, maybe his secretary, too.

A bright light flashed from above. He leaned forward in his chair, looking up. It looked like a hoverambulance jetting away.

He heard their arguing steadily grow louder. His weapon was ready when they appeared from the left, about ten feet from his entrance, and moved further away. It was a man and a woman yelling at each other.

Beta Max couldn't help but smile as the man and woman disappeared around the corner of shacks right out of view. He could still hear them as the noise got lower and lower, until the yelling was gone. His weapon was returned to his lap without the death grip.

The black hovercar appeared again, but this time, it was not speeding. It coasted by until it was out of view again. He knew it stopped. He heard doors open and close.

He saw them: silhouettes in the distance, at first, and then they came into the light. Caret was on the left, and Logo on the right. The men casually walked towards the open doors, as if they knew, or saw, they were wide open. It was as if they were looking directly at him.

Beta Max stood from his chair in the dark. This was it. She'd told.

Caret engaged his new light sword. Logo pulled his laser gun from his jacket.

Beta Max walked out of the shack to face them, gun in hand. He would wait until he could see the whites of their eyes before firing.

There was a sonic blast in the air. None of them knew what it was, or where it had come from. The men stopped, looking up, completely startled.

"This is the police! Drop your weapons and freeze! Or you will be fired on and killed!"

Silver and black jetpacked police personnel descended from the dark sky around the men. Police cruisers seemed to appear from nowhere. In moments, all three men were handcuffed.

Caret, smiling, and Logo, with a deep frown, watched Beta Max. Beta Max started laughing.

They were all dragged away to separate police cruisers. Soon they would be at Police One, and the beginning of the end would commence, courtesy of the Metro criminal justice system.

CHAPTER 67

Cruz, the Interrogator

Interrogate? I was a civilian, and there was no way Metropolis Police would let me talk to someone in interrogation. I asked to be allowed to ask a few questions, but they didn't even want me in the room.

All three of the gangsters had been interrogated for half the day, but none of the men had uttered a word. Neither threats nor deals had made them budge. However, none of the men had asked for their attorneys, either. I made my case. This time, they listened.

"I thought we were friends, Cruz," Beta Max said to me.

That was the compromise. I couldn't talk to all three of them. I had to pick one.

Beta Max was restrained to the table, and I sat across from him.

"Yes, I'm sorry. I shouldn't have told Caret and Logo that you were the one who tried to kill them, and not each other. How was I to know you were all such good friends, going way back? Maybe being your friend isn't the best thing for one to be."

"I'm hurt, Cruz." He was talking! "But you did save me from them. If you hadn't called, I would've been done for. Then you saved me again. See, Cruz, we are friends."

"You know it was her, not them. I heard you had some trouble with killers at your offices too. That wasn't Caret or Logo."

"It was."

"How could they have been sent by them if Caret and Logo didn't know you were the one who'd tried to kill them yet? You sent your killers to get them. She sent her killers to get you. Tying up all her loose ends, but you knew that already."

Beta Max was quiet for a moment. "Yes, I did."

"I think you need to give us what we need, to end all this. You and your friends won't be going anywhere, but don't you think she should be here too?"

"She's smarter than you, Cruz, smarter than me, smarter than all of us. It was my idea, but she took my idea, and made it bigger. You think you know all the pieces, but you don't."

"Tell me, then."

"What does it matter? When enough pieces have been removed from a thing, it's no longer what it could have been. What does it matter what it was going to be? You've figured out enough. It's over."

"Only one loose end left."

"Yes, one." He smiled. "I wonder if you'll get her, or she'll get you. Or maybe you'll both end up dead at each other's hands. These are the only three choices left for you, Mr. Cruz. Make it count."

PART NINE

A Dame to Die For

CHAPTER 68

I, Executioner

We left Metro PD, and made one stop. On reflection, it could have been a fatal and final mistake for me. We went back to the Liquid Cool office for additional firepower. I had PJ close the office, and go home, but we were there. It was clearly one the dumbest things I had ever done as a private detective, especially knowing my arch-nemesis was after me.

I was in my private office, with my sidewalk sallies next to me, when we heard the commotion. It was like nothing we'd heard before. The sound was like some unstoppable force had shot out from the elevator we'd just been in, crashed into the walls of the hallway, and was wrecking its way toward Liquid Cool.

Something smashed through the front door of the main office. My sidewalk sallies were aiming their guns at my partly closed inside office, at whatever was coming, with fear in their faces. Instead of reaching for a weapon, I quickly opened my desk, and then pushed a secret button to pop open a secret compartment. I was about to use the special device

Bugs had given me when I'd first had him enhance the security of my offices.

I had come across a killer robot in my last case, I'd been chased by killer robot dogs in the one before that, but the killer robot that rumbled into the offices, shaking the ground as it walked, was an illegal wrecker-model that was programmed to do one and one thing only—kill me and anyone with me. It was a cube-like humanoid, with a large mirrored eye, and ten fingers on each of its pile-driver arms. We could see the tips of its fingers begin to glow as it lurched forward.

I pressed the button of the tiny device in my hand as fast as I could. The EMP shock wave was not painful. The effect only lasted a moment, but when we looked up, the killer robot was stopped dead—every light off, every circuit fried.

We didn't even want to know what the NeuroDancer's killer robot would have done to us.

CHAPTER 69

The NeuroDancer

Beta Max ratted her out.

We had expected him to say she was hiding in some Free City hovel somewhere. Beta Max seemed to know all the Free City nooks and crannies to hide in. But no, the NeuroDancer was living out of a pleasure penthouse in Silicon Dunes. She was still a world-famous dance star. Why shouldn't she be hiding out in the highest class of comfort? She surely had the money for it. We were the only ones who knew she was also a megalomaniacal psycho.

With my two main sidewalk sallies in tow, we were off.

It was tricky, because this was technically a police investigation. Police don't let civilians do their work. But I had caused another Red Ball (high-profile, top priority action), and police were all over Metropolis arresting people: Beta Max's people, the VTV people, and NeuroDancer's people, whether they were under suspicion or not. They wanted everyone arrested. NeuroDancer was spotted at one of her favorite restaurants, so they gave me the green light to secure her apartment, until they could get there.

Chief Hub basically wanted me out of Police Central as quickly as possible. When I was leaving, I saw why. The media was descending upon the station like a swarm. He didn't even want me to be seen, which was fine by me.

We were in the Pony, and were gone—again. I was the one who insisted we stop at Liquid Cool in Buzz Town. My sidewalk sallies told me to go straight to Silicon Dunes. I could have gotten all of us killed.

"Why was Phishy messing around with my driver's seat settings?" I asked, when we first left Metro PD.

I had to reset everything. Phishy wouldn't be driving the Pony again.

We all had the same reaction. Whenever you went to a place to get someone, and there was the person standing there, waiting for you, with their hands in their pockets, there was only one reaction. Holy Crap!

When I saw her standing there in the room, waiting, I knew we had been played in the best possible way. Everything Beta Max had given us was true; otherwise, we wouldn't have believed it. Otherwise, I wouldn't have walked right into her final trap. Beta Max was not a boyfriend scorned. He was playing the final role in her contingency plan. It was all part of her clean-up plan. The NeuroDancer had one last thing to do before making her final getaway. Did she know I'd killed her robot at my office?

"In all this time," she said, "I could never figure out how you figured it out, Mr. Cruz. At the very beginning, you knew I was the woman behind the curtain, controlling it all. You were so certain, never wavered. You couldn't have known from the beginning. How could you? You didn't know who I was. You never met me before. You never investigated me. You never asked anyone about me. When you finally did, it was near the end of everything, but you had long since formed your opinions in stone. How could you have known I was your arch-villain nemesis? You didn't even know me."

"You told me."

"What?"

"It was like a tune in my head, 'I am your arch-villain nemesis'. Over and over, it played in my head. I didn't know what it meant, and why it kept popping up in my head. It wasn't until my friends saved me from my rooftop dancing and near-header off the edge that I figured it out. When you did whatever you did to me in my office, before I left for my wedding, you probably were talking. Weren't you? You were probably gloating, and said it to me as an exercise of your criminal superiority. 'I am your arch-villain nemesis.' You said that, didn't you? I talked to a psycho-hypnotist to find out the term. Post-hypnotic suggestion, it's called. That's what you did, and didn't even realize what you were doing. You created your own arch-hero nemesis, and didn't even realize it. I told you that in the hallway. That's your fatal flaw. You don't know how to keep your mouth shut. *You* were the one who put me on to you, before anything ever started."

I could see the realization of what she had done come over her face. Then came the simmering rage. She remained calm, but inside, I knew her anger was like a nuclear bomb exploding.

"Do you know, Mr. Cruz, I saved your life once, before I tried to end it?" Oh, no, I thought. The upper-class, faux British accent was gone. She was speaking in her normal voice. The entire act was over. Criminals did that for one reason only. "That man outside your office, that day, would have shot you dead, but I took care of him—had him simply follow me into the elevator down like a puppy. I wanted to see the 'famous' detective work, see how far you'd get, what you'd uncover. Don't hate me because I was curious." She laughed. "If I had only been able to see the future."

"The bad guy saves the good guy who takes her down. Shakespearean, I believe they call it."

"Tragic is what they call it—for you. Computer companies are known to create vulnerabilities in their own software, because they want the hackers to go down a certain pathway. Security firms purposely create vulnerabilities in their security systems, because they want the thieves to breach it at only a certain point. They control the access ways, so they can control the trespasser and catch them. I purposely created the trail of bread crumbs for someone to follow and trap themselves for me. I never thought I was creating it for you."

"You can't rule the galaxy if you can only control the men," I said.

"You didn't think I could only control the men, did you?"

She didn't give me a chance to continue the banter.

Actually, I'd never believed her mind-control ability was over men only. I'd just wanted her to think I believed that. When she came to the Liquid Cool offices with her male stripper dancers, she was putting on a show. When I was waiting there, flanked by my sidewalk sally bodyguards, I was putting on a show—for her.

I was staring up at the ceiling. I blinked a few times; it was as if I were coming out of unconsciousness, as if I had fainted. Something was still pushing my left shoulder. I finally turned, and it was Sidewalk Sally Jane. She was shot in the shoulder, but her eyes were open.

I turned to my other side, and Sidewalk Sally Teal was bad. I jumped up, and ran over to her. She was unconsciousness, and shot in the side. The bulletproof vest under her blouse had protected her chest fine, but that's not where she'd been shot. I checked for a pulse, and she had one, though it seemed weak. I had to call for an ambulance.

I saw her. As I stood up to get my mobile out of my jacket to call the police, I stepped to her. I noticed that my omega-gun, uniquely attached, had engaged, and was hanging off my right arm. If I moved too fast, its muzzle touched my open skin and burned it.

The NeuroDancer was on her back, a blank stare at the ceiling above. My omega-gun had blown a hole straight through her upper body, and blown the top part of her forehead clean off. We both had been clever, but I was the one standing, and she was the one stone cold dead on the floor.

She could have pulled it all off, but the sheer magnitude of the scheme was her undoing, not me. If she had just wanted a studio, to siphon off all its money for her own purposes, she would have succeeded. If she'd wanted to control the supercity with her own zombie politicians, she could have possibly succeeded. If she wanted to control all the VR zombies in the world even, she might have succeeded—but not all three. Not to mention the Gangsters' Graveyard, which showed the premeditated evil of her plan. Those she couldn't control, she was going to make disappear. It was too much—too brazen, too grandiose, too evil.

Who knew that pillow talk could lead to a grand scheme so diabolical? Caret, Logo, Jed, and Beta Max let slip their individual plans to the wrong woman. She wasn't performing for them; they were performing for her—NeuroDancer's rats in her maze, but without the flashy, plenty-of-skin, high-fashion dance outfits.

Even if things had been reversed, if she were standing and I were the dead piece of meat on the ground, would she have won? Against me, yes, but that was not her ambition. It was to rule the galaxy. The little dance performer had no idea what sinister creatures in human form existed on Earth, and Up-Top. She would have come to her end soon, in any of a million different ways: the Council of Corporations, sinister shadow groups and megacorporations, Up-Top, even Metropolis, itself, was a supercity too big to be controlled by any one person. She would have ended herself by one of them, even if I hadn't.

People wanted to rule the world, rule humankind. She wouldn't be the last megalomaniac by a long shot. There would always be a never-ending stream of bad guys—and gals. However, the universe always made sure there was a never-ending stream of good guys to stop them.

Her funeral was fit for a King and Queen. People mourned the death of NeuroDancer for months on end. I suspected it would go on for years, and the day would be a permanent day of mourning on the calendar. Metropolis wisely, and luckily for me, listed her death as an accidental overdose of drugs. No one, even in her inner circle, questioned the City Coroner's office. It was easy enough to reconstruct the body for a public viewing, which was done. Metropolis wanted her, and the whole thing, buried as quickly as the public would allow.

The three gangsters would never see the light of day. There was more than enough evidence to link them to each of the three separate scandals. The fourth gangster, Jed, had unwisely resurfaced after I'd had him tucked away, and tried to escape to Up-Top. He didn't count on us flagging his DNA at every terminal. He was picked up, and he too, had enough evidence left behind, as with the others, courtesy of the NeuroDancer, to send him away forever—linking him to the Gangsters' Graveyard plot.

I still didn't know why they'd wanted the hoverbike helmet in Caret's father's possession so badly. I was never going to give it to them. If they wanted it, then it was dangerous, even if I didn't how. I decided to keep it in a safety security box for now. I would either figure it out later—or not. Caret Senior really was mentally unstable, so he wasn't going to be leaving Metro Asylum anytime soon. I often wondered if his condition was a result of being one of NeuroDancer's first mind-control "test subjects."

It was all wrapped up nicely. I had sold that fully completed screenplay to Mrs. Meta, who became her own movie studio head for the coming rebirth of Movie-Town. Her tenure didn't last long, because she had the "brilliant" idea that all live actors should be abolished, and computer-generated ones should be used in movies instead. Well, she got the boot, but it didn't affect my deal for the project.

No one in the public would ever know about the Prime Numbers scandal. Special secret panels were convened, and the decision was made to let all the election results stand. All losing candidates were notified, and after many closed-door discussions, none of them contested it. I wondered what they threatened or blackmailed them with.

The VR scandal was easy. Tell no one, and move on. None of the billions of players would ever know they could have become mind-controlled zombies. There, at least, NeuroDancer would live forever, as a virtual person in the endless VR games and worlds on Earth, as well as Up-Top.

Before the hoverambulance arrived for my sidewalk sally team, Run-Time's people—Bugs and his men—checked over the Dame's body and belongings. They scanned everything. Nothing. No devices or any clue as to how she did what she did to me and the sidewalk sallies in that office. The answer to the mystery of her mind-control powers had died with her. There would be a full autopsy by Metro coroners, and I contrived a way to get in to view the reports, but they never turned up anything either. The secret would die with her, and that was okay with me. As long as no one else got her ability or, even better, knew about it. The megacorps and governments would kill, and more, to control such tech.

As I looked out the window of my 100th floor office, I saw a VTV hoverdirigible. The communications megacorp had been cleared of any illegality, but not of suspicion, by more people than just me. On the side of the air-vehicle was a digital advertisement of their VTV products. They would not be thwarted in their quest to get one of their VTVs in every home in Metropolis and beyond.

Was that the real reason for the NeuroDancer's first visit to my office, that fateful day? The VTV hoverdirigibles were all over the Metropolis skies, including right in front of the Liquid Cool building, daily. Maybe, she heard of my ability to figure things out, and feared it. Since she had lots of boyfriends, maybe she knew I would be meeting with Caret, Logo, Jed, and Beta Max one day, and wanted to take a piece of the puzzle off the table. I still remembered my visit to Beta Max's Silver City facility as Mr. Incom, and my strange inability to see the words "VTV" on the reps I'd bumped into—my brain was blocking it out—and now I knew the affliction was NeuroDancer's doing. It didn't matter anymore. I had still figured it out—all the pieces that mattered.

It was over. I had just spent all my money on repairing the damage to the Pony from my two movie star actor assassins, and the Liquid Cool offices again, after the killer robot attack.

The final close to the case would be New Vegas. We had already had the big wedding, with the folks, and the million relatives, but I was "under the influence" of the NeuroDancer. It was like a dark, rancid cloud over my special day. Even Dot wasn't happy about that. So, we loaded up the Pony—Dot, Run-Time, Phishy (who would get his long-sought-after title of "second best man"), PJ, and me—and off we went to New Vegas for the drive-through wedding with an Elvis priest. We couldn't, and wouldn't, redo the full wedding, but we could redo a simple one. There's no law against marrying the same person more than once. That's what we did one Saturday night. With Dot and I saying "I do," the kiss, PJ throwing bouquets with her buff bionic arms, Phishy showering everyone with rice, we all mentally closed the Case of the NeuroDancer forever.

Thank you for reading!

Dear Reader,

I hope you enjoyed my **Liquid Cool** cyberpunk detective novel, *NeuroDancer*.

Can You Write Me a Review?

If you enjoyed ***NeuroDancer*** *(Liquid Cool, Book 3)*, I'd greatly appreciate an honest review on one or more of the following sites:

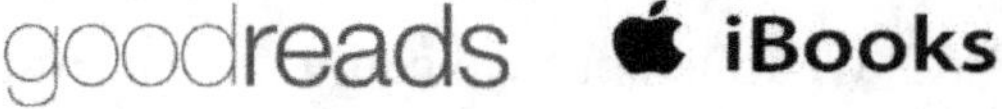

Reviews are the best way for readers to discover good books. My writer's motto is simple: "Readers Rule!" Thanks so much.

Always writing,

Austin Dragon

CONTINUE THE ADVENTURE

Get Your Next *Liquid Cool* Books!

- ***These Mean Streets, Darkly*** *(Liquid Cool Prequel Short)*
- ***Liquid Cool*** *(Liquid Cool: The Cyberpunk Detective Series, Book 1)*
- ***Blade Gunner*** *(Liquid Cool, Book 2)*
- ***NeuroDancer*** *(Liquid Cool, Book 3)*
- ***The Electric Sheep Massacre*** *(Liquid Cool, Book 4)*
- ***I, Alien Hunter*** *(Liquid Cool, Book 5)*
- ***A.I. Confidential*** *(Liquid Cool, Book 6)*

- ***Liquid Cool Box Set*** *(Liquid Cool Prequel and Books 1-3)*
- ***Liquid Cool Box Set 2*** *(Liquid Cool: Books 4-6)*

Also by Austin Dragon

See all my books in science fiction, horror, and fantasy at: http://www.austindragon.com/books

ABOUT THE AUTHOR

Austin Dragon is the author of the *After Eden Series*, including the mini-series, *After Eden: Tek-Fall*, the classic *Sleepy Hollow Horrors*, the new epic fantasy adventure *Fabled Quest Chronicles*, and the cyberpunk detective series, *Liquid Cool*. He is a native New Yorker, but has called Los Angeles, California home for the last twenty years. Words to describe him, in no particular order: U.S. Army, English teacher, one-time resident of Paris, political junkie, movie buff, Fortune 500 corporate recruiter, renaissance man, dreamer.

He is currently working on new books and series in science fiction, fantasy, and classic horror!

Connect with Austin on social media at:

Website and blog: http://www.austindragon.com

Twitter: https://twitter.com/Austin_Dragon

Pinterest: http://www.pinterest.com/austindragon

Google+: https://google.com/+AustinDragonAuthor

Goodreads: https://www.goodreads.com/ADragon

Other books by Austin:
See all my books at: **http://www.austindragon.com/books**

9 781946 590565